Special thanks to:

Alex, Allison Grier, Arne Radtke, Beth Lear VanderYacht, Chad Bowden, Charlotte, Chris Meeson, Dave Baxter, David Lars Chamberlain, Elias Rosner, Erica Hecker, Erica Jordan, Gerald P. McDaniel, Greywolfe, Janice Jurgens, Jeff Lewis, John "AcesofDeath7" Mullens, Joshua Bowers, Khadija Hussain, Lisa Lyons, Maxi Organ, Michael Di Salvo, NeonPixxius, Pascal Dieter Beuer, Paul Popernack, Rob MacAndrew, Scott Kilburn, Sky Fallows, Todd Good, Victoria Nohelty, and Walter Weiss.

ALSO BY RUSSELL NOHELTY

THE GODVERSE CHRONICLES
And Death Followed Behind Her
And Doom Followed Behind Her
And Ruin Followed Behind Her
And Hell Followed Behind Her
Katrina Hates the Dead
Pixie Dust

OTHER NOVEL WORK
My Father Didn't Kill Himself
Sorry for Existing
Gumshoes: The Case of Madison's Father
The Invasion Saga
The Vessel
Worst Thing in the Universe
The Void Calls Us Home
The Marked Ones
The Sleeping Beauty

OTHER ILLUSTRATED WORK
The Little Bird and the Little Worm
Ichabod Jones: Monster Hunter
Gherkin Boy

www.russellnohelty.com

Anna and the Dark Place

By:

Russell Nohelty

Edited by:

Leah Lederman

Proofread by:

Katrina Roets

Cover by:

Paramita Bhattacharjee

Chapter 1

Funerals suck.

That wasn't some great revelation or anything, but just because it wasn't profound didn't make it any less true. I wasn't trying to be Shakespeare. Every word out of my mouth or thought in my head didn't need to be some pithy observation meant to entertain a billion people for a thousand years.

In my short sixteen years of life, I'd been to four funerals, though, so I knew something about the subject: all of them sucked, hard. I wasn't a mob hitman. Why had I been to so many funerals at such a tender age? Some people chalked it up to bad luck, but I had the sneaking suspicion I was cursed.

The first funeral I attended was for my nana. She was old, and I was three. I couldn't remember that one very well because…well, I was three. Who remembers anything from when they were three? Nobody, that's who.

Next was my Aunt Pauline. She smoked a pack of cigarettes a day until the day she died. I wasn't surprised she died young, but I was surprised she could afford the habit even after they raised the price to over seven dollars a pack. I guess it was lucky that she retired rich with the right stock options. Or maybe it wasn't lucky, since those cigarettes killed her.

The third funeral was my father's, and it sucked super hard. Kids are supposed to outlive their parents, but that didn't make it suck any less. Parents were supposed to die after they'd gotten older, like when they were ninety, not when they were forty-five.

Although, maybe I need to shut my mouth, because it's better to outlive your parent than to have your parent outlive you.

Katie was my best friend, and the owner of the body that was being lowered into the ground in front of me. We had known each other all of our lives. Our parents brought us home from the hospital within a month of each other, and our fathers left us at the same time, both through the same helicopter accident in Kabul which killed their whole unit.

Crap. I had been to five funerals. I forgot that Katie's father had a funeral the day after my father's, so they blended together.

Katie and I grew up across the street from each other, and our families did everything together, from having barbecues, to watching the Super Bowl, to going on vacations together. After our fathers died, Katie and Joanne became even closer to us. We didn't have much family left. My father was an only child, and my mother only had Pauline. Once they were gone, and Nana too, our family became just my mother, me, Katie, and Joanne.

I hated death with a real passion, too. It wasn't fair. All the other kids had brothers, sisters, cousins, aunts, uncles, fathers, grandparents…they had a family. They had friends. They had support.

Death took all of that away from me. Every person I grew close to faded out of my life. After my father died, I stopped letting people in. I walled myself off from the outside world. I figured if everybody was going to die, and it hurt so bad every time they did, at least I could be hurt by as few people as possible.

I didn't join any clubs, or play any sports, or go to any parties. All I did was come home after school and hang out with Katie, and whatever friends she bothered to bring around me. She never had the same fears I did, despite death taking her father away just like it had mine.

She was the opposite of me. After her father's death, Katie decided to go out into the world and meet new people. She signed up for all the clubs and never met a person she didn't like. She lived more in her few years on this planet than most people, and certainly had more of a life than I ever did.

Joanne stood from her seat next to mine in the cemetery and walked up to the podium beside Katie's grave. Her hair was once blonde and vibrant, but she long ago let it return to its natural brown, which matched her eyes. Her skin was white and pale, and her eyes were red from crying.

"Thank you for coming," Joanne said, as her daughter was lowered into the grave in front of her. "I know it's not normal to give the eulogy at the cemetery instead of a church, but my Katie wasn't normal, either."

Katie had planned her own funeral, which was how I learned that the difference between a cemetery and a graveyard is that a graveyard is connected to a church and a cemetery isn't connected to anything. Katie hated churches, and she refused to be buried in a graveyard. She wanted her funeral to take place outdoors, not in some stuffy funeral parlor.

Joanne wiped the tears from her eyes. "Katie told me the day she was diagnosed that she was going to die, but that didn't stop her from fighting anyway."

It was true. I was there. Specifically, what she said was, "Mom, I don't think I'm going to beat this cancer, but I'm not going down without a fight." That was the kind of person Katie was, practical but headstrong. She ended up being right too, about her death at least, which I hated her for just a little bit, which made me love her just 9,999,999 percent more than anybody else.

"She wasn't scared of death," Joanne continued, choking on her tears. "Even in the last days of her life, she saw it as another step in the journey. She didn't know where she was going to go, but she knew it would be a better place."

That part was a lie, but at least it was only a lie of omission. She said it wouldn't be any worse of a place, or at least that's what she told me. She could have said something different to her mother. Then, she only would have been lying to one of us, but Katie always believed that lies were okay as long as they came from a place of kindness.

"I know she's in a better place." Joanne paused, swallowing her tears. "And one day we will be together again in the next life. Until then, Katie would have wanted me to live. She would have wanted us all to live; to embrace life, and to cherish every day as if it were our last."

That did sound like her. Hopelessly optimistic even in the end, even when she had no reason to be optimistic. "Cheer up," she would tell me whenever I visited her in the hospital during her chemo treatments. "I'm the one dying."

She was wrong, of course. We were all the ones dying. She was just dying sooner than the rest of us. One day we would all be dead. What would happen to me then? Would I really be reunited with Katie, or would I just rot in the ground?

Joanne grabbed a rose from the foldout table next to her. There were over a hundred roses piled there. I looked around and there were only a few dozen people in attendance, but that was Katie, always hopelessly optimistic, even about how many people would attend her funeral.

I helped Katie plan her funeral, once the tumors in her bones became inoperable. She wanted me to put a clown nose on her, and make sure everybody honked it when they passed. It was the only thing Joanne refused to do for her after she died. It was a shame, because that was a perfectly Katie moment, laughing at death and making everybody around her feel slightly less uncomfortable.

After a moment of silent contemplation, Joanne turned to us again. "Now, please step forward and send my daughter into the afterlife with a rose."

I walked forward with my mother and picked up three roses, then headed slowly toward the grave where the coffin was already lowered.

"I wish we had more time together," I whispered. I threw the roses into the hole in the ground which held my best friend's body. "Goodbye."

Chapter 2

Katie had hundreds of friends before she was diagnosed with leukemia. They came to sleepovers at her house and cheered her on during soccer games. Everybody said they loved her. People loved Katie…but then she became sick. Once she got sick, the number of friends she had whittled down until there was just me again.

It was the best part of Katie being sick, honestly. I finally got to hang out with her without a gaggle of other friends around. Most of middle school saw me watching from the sidelines as Katie did one amazing thing after another, leaving me behind little by little. She kept me around once she became popular, but it was never the same as when we were younger.

Don't get me wrong. I absolutely hated that Katie had cancer, but that didn't mean it was without its benefits. Most things, no matter how horrible, had tangential benefits. Hell, they say Hitler kept the trains running on time, but that doesn't mean anybody wanted another Holocaust.

Everybody abandoned Katie once the cancer got hard, and she stopped being peppy all the time, which meant she needed a friend. A real friend. Somebody who wouldn't complain when she couldn't go out on Friday night. One that held her hair when she threw up and who told her she looked good when all that hair came out during the horrible days after chemo when all she wanted to do was cry and sleep.

I was glad that person was me. We would stay up late at night, read books together, and talk about life and the universe, just like when we were kids. I never begrudged Katie her accolades or friendships. I really, seriously wanted what was best for her. I never wanted her to be sick and hoped against hope that she was wrong about dying. It turned out everything she said would happen, did happen.

I ended up in Katie's room an hour after the funeral, looking out at my pale, purple house across the street. It sorely needed a paint job. Every night, Katie and I would say goodnight to each other through our windows, and every morning I would rush to the window to make sure she was still alive.

When I woke up on the day she died, her mother was in her room, crying. I watched her scream and collapse on her daughter's lifeless corpse. I knew what had happened, but that didn't stop me from running across the street and pushing open the front door that Joanne never locked.

Katie didn't look dead when I saw her the morning after she died. She was pale, but she had been paling for months, and she was so skinny in the final months of her life that I could see her bones through her sagging skin. Her blonde hair had long ago fallen out, and her dark blue eyes were closed as if she were sleeping.

She died in her sleep, and I wasn't there to comfort her. Nobody was there for her in those final moments.

I was likely the last person to see her alive. Her mother had kissed her goodnight and tucked her in before we waved to each other that night. Had I known it would be the last time I saw her, I would have said more; I would have told her how I really felt about her, but I had no clue she would be dead by morning.

"She really loved you, Anna," Joanne said from the doorway behind me.

I turned around and collapsed into her arms. "I know. I loved her too."

We didn't move for a long time, except for our chests, which heaved in pain against each other. Eventually, when the tears were gone, I unlatched from her. I wiped the tears from my eyes and gave her the smallest of smiles.

"Come downstairs," Joanne said. "I can't do this alone."

"In a minute," I replied.

I wanted to help Joanne, but crowds…I didn't like crowds, and I didn't like when they fawned over a girl they barely knew. More so, I hated the fact that they were all still alive and Katie wasn't. It was a horrible thought, but I just wanted my friend back. Seeing all of them alive, smiling, and being with the ones they loved, was too much for me to take.

I sat down on Katie's bed and fell onto her pillow. I could smell her shampoo. The sweet smell of roses and vanilla filled my nostrils, and for a moment Katie was alive again in my memory. I thought the tears were gone, but I was wrong. My body convulsed again, and they came back harder than ever.

Why? Katie. Why did you leave me?

It was a selfish thought, but it was a true one. I wept for Katie, for all the potential she lost, and all the days she would no longer have, but in that moment, I wept because I would never see her again. I wept because of what her death did to me.

I once had three people I loved in this world. My mother, Joanne, and Katie. Now I only had two. And I didn't love them as much as I loved Katie.

Chapter 3

I didn't want to sleep in my room any more. My room faced Katie's, across the street, and that meant memories of her flooded into my brain every time I looked out my window. I had taken to sleeping on the couch in the living room, and only sleeping with Netflix blaring *Parks and Rec* on repeat. Otherwise, the dark thoughts infested my brain.

Why couldn't you save her?

Why didn't you die?

What makes you so special?

These questions filled my brain, and I couldn't answer them. I had no idea why Katie couldn't be saved, and why I was alive while so many people I loved died.

Was I the toxic piece that killed everyone around me? Was I a mold, or a spore, that infected those I cared about? Or was I just unlucky that my love was met by death at every turn. I long ago decided never to love again, but perhaps that wasn't enough. Perhaps I needed to curtail the love I had for those still alive. Maybe it was in their best interests if I just cut off all ties and ran away.

"Move over," Mom said to me, sitting down on the couch.

"Mom," I said. "I'm trying to sleep."

"Too bad," she replied. "There's a TV in your room. You can use it if you want, but this one is the family TV."

I kicked her lightly, trying to get her up, but she wasn't moving. "I have school in the morning."

"You have a bed for that, my love. Now, what are we watching?"

I sighed. "Parks and Rec, I guess."

"All right, I can dig it. Which season?"

"Three."

"Ooh, that's a good one. Before or after April and Andy's wedding?"

"I don't know," I said. "It's just background noise."

She stared at the TV for a moment. "Before, definitely before. Come on, sit up. Your bony legs are poking into my side."

I pulled my legs up and Mom fell back onto the couch. "I hate you."

She rubbed my legs gently. "No, you don't. Sometimes maybe you wish you did, but you don't."

I couldn't argue with her. There wasn't anything in the world that could make me stop loving Mom, even if she was cursed to die eventually, just like everyone else I loved. It was just a matter of time.

"You realize if I don't sleep then I won't be fresh for school tomorrow?"

"Yeah, I know," she said. "But there's nothing I can do about that, besides forklift you upstairs, and I'm afraid they won't let me take one home."

Mom had the strong hands and wide build of a warehouse worker. Lots of people made fun of her when she went to work in the warehouse after Dad died, but it was one of the few places that paid decently enough for us to keep the house they'd bought before I was born. They didn't want to hire her at first, but soon enough, she proved herself, and eventually they promoted her to warehouse manager. After a few years she might even get promoted to the day shift.

"Don't you have work?" I said.

"My boss is a real dick, but even she wouldn't make me work the night of my friend's funeral."

"Aren't you the boss, though?" I asked.

"There's still the owner over me," she said, then sighed. "There's always a boss over you."

"Sure, but you work the night crew. Do you think they're really up to check on you?"

"No, but I'm also very self-aware. And I'm also aware when my kid doesn't want to sleep in her own room because she doesn't want to be reminded of her friend."

"So, you're a psychologist now?" I asked.

"No, but someday, maybe."

Mom was studying psychology in community college. She hoped one day to transfer to get a four-year degree, but right now it meant she was hardly ever home between school and work. Luckily, I was very self-reliant. I had been a latchkey kid for a long time, and so she could trust me to be home alone.

I scooted back on the couch and swung my legs off it. "I can't, Mom. I can't be reminded of her."

"I know, sweetie," she replied. "We both loved her, you know."

I nodded. "I know you did. She was like a daughter to you."

"She was a daughter to me, just like you're a daughter to Joanne. It's never easy to lose a daughter, or a father, or a husband. That piece of your soul, it will never come back."

"Does it get easier?" I asked. "I thought it would get easier after Daddy, but it's just as hard. It's always just as hard."

"Some days will be easier than others. This day has been brutally hard, my love. But some days will be easy, and some days you will feel guilty about how easy it becomes, and it will make you spiral."

"You are not a very good psychologist, Mom."

"I'm only in my first year. Freud wasn't Freud on day one."

"No, not until he found cocaine. That's when he became Freud."

"All right, smarty-pants, we can all Wikipedia. That doesn't make you smart."

"No," I replied. "The straight A's make me smart."

"That just makes you book smart, kiddo." Mom pulled my head close to hers and kissed my forehead. "That doesn't make you street smart, and that doesn't make you heart smart, either."

"Now you sound like a Lipitor commercial."

"Just shut up and watch your show, okay?"

I snuggled into Mom's stomach and turned to the TV. I listened to her heart beat against my ear, and it slowly lulled me off to sleep. How could I ever stop loving my mother? She knew exactly what I needed. I didn't need compassion, or pity. I just needed somebody to be there, and act like everything was normal, even when nothing was, and nothing would ever be again.

Chapter 4

The first day back at school after Katie's death was the worst. She hadn't been at school most of the year, but the thought of seeing her when I got home kept me going every day. I didn't have that spark of joy anymore, and now I was alone.

I didn't have a lot of friends before I lost her but going back into that school just showed me how alone I truly was without Katie by my side. I had always fed off her glow, and she glowed so brightly it rubbed off on me. It made it seem like I glowed, too, especially in my darkest moments. There wasn't any more glow. Just the creeping darkness.

As I walked to class, my eyes caught Rebecca Swinton chatting with the rest of Katie's friends. Rebecca was the queen bee of school, and used to be Katie's best friend, besides me, of course. When Katie got sick and she stopped coming to school, Rebecca stopped coming to see her before long. She didn't come to Katie's funeral, either. None of them did.

I was going to walk past her, just like I always did, but my stomach boiled over with the thought of her snubbing Katie's funeral.

"It was a nice service," I said, sneering at her as I passed.

"Excuse me?" Rebecca said.

"Katie's funeral," I replied, clenching my jaw. "I thought you should know, since you were such a good friend. So good a friend you couldn't even show up."

"Shut up, freak," Rebecca said. "We sent flowers. I just…couldn't go…okay?"

"I'm sure you had a busy schedule." I turned away from her and walked down the hall. I couldn't deal with her. I never could deal with her, but I tried for Katie.

Katie never would have been so mean to Rebecca. She would have understood why she didn't come to the funeral. That was why everybody loved Katie so much. Or was it because they fed on her glow like I did? Maybe we were all just junkies, trying to get as much of her as we could while she was alive.

I felt a tap on my shoulder. I turned around to see Stephanie, one of Rebecca's horde, and another person who missed the funeral. She smiled a crooked smile at me as she shifted from one foot to the other on her shiny clogs.

"So…you were there?" Stephanie asked me. Her normally bouncy, blonde hair was disheveled and flat. "At the funeral?"

"I was there," I replied, trying to brush past her. "It was lovely."

"I wanted to go. I just couldn't go. I had reasons."

"I'm sure she understands," I said. "Just like how you couldn't see her during her last round of chemo."

"I tried to go. It was just so sad."

"It was sad. It was horrible. She threw up every day for a week. She couldn't talk. She withered away alone, with just me. I'm sure she can forgive you for not coming to her funeral, but I'll never forgive you for not coming to see her."

"I just…couldn't."

"Yeah, none of you could."

I slammed my shoulder against hers and she spun around. Katie wouldn't approve of me being so hard on

Stephanie, or any of them. She didn't want anybody to come unless they wanted to be there. She always said that she didn't hold it against them.

But I held it against myself, because the truth was, I didn't want them to come. I didn't want them to see her. I wanted Katie all to myself, and that was selfish. Now, every time I saw Stephanie, or Amber, or Rebecca, that's all I was going to be able to think about, how I prayed every single night that they wouldn't come see her, so I could have Katie all to myself. The worst part was, with Katie gone, they were the only thing I had left to remember her in this horrible place.

I was doing it again. Making it all about myself, but that's all I have left now, myself. Walking down the halls of school, alone, just like I had so many times before. But this time was different because I knew in my bones Katie wouldn't be back, ever. No matter how much I hoped for her return.

Chapter 5

I walked into first period and took my usual seat next to Katie's empty desk. Even when she had been too busy to hang out with me, we always sat next to each other in first period English and caught up on the gossip of the day. It was our perfect, little oasis from the rest of life. Now, it was nothing but an inanimate object that held hundreds of memories of Katie.

"Sit down, class!" Mrs. Hooper said from the front of the room. She was a tall woman, and slender, with wild hair like she was caught in a tornado and never bothered to fix herself up afterwards. She retained that aesthetic: from her windswept hair down to her cockeyed glasses, through her wrinkled lime-green dress, and down to her mismatched socks. She was a train wreck disaster, but she was our train wreck. English was the only class Katie and I enjoyed, mostly because we could enjoy it together.

"Class," Mrs. Hooper yelled again. "Settle down."

How could she expect teenagers to settle down first thing in the morning? There was so much to discuss, and so much energy to dispel. My fellow classmates shuffled loudly to their seats, scooting in their metal chairs with all the grace of a herd of water buffaloes.

"We have a new student with us today," Mrs. Hooper said. The class responded with a chorus of groans. "I know it's already crowded in here, but we're just going to have to make do."

Budget cuts whittled down our teachers and ballooned our class sizes until the classrooms were all bursting at the seams with students. Luckily, I didn't mind being lost in the cacophony of other students. I was just as happy to be overlooked in a big group as I was in a small one. Of course, Katie never let that happen when she could help it. She always tried to get me involved, even when all I wanted to do was slouch down in my chair and be forgotten.

"Anna Aguilar!" Mrs. Hooper called out.

"Present," I said, though I was hesitant. Nothing good came from the teacher calling on you.

"Can you raise your hand, please?" Mrs. Hooper called out. I was being blocked by Butch, the star linebacker of the football team and my personal barrier from ever being called on by the teacher except when Katie singled me out.

"It's already raised," I said, waving my hand back and forth.

Mrs. Hooper looked around the room. "Can you stand, then?"

I pushed my desk out and stood up. Standing next to the teacher was a short girl with dark skin and thick, circular glasses. She wore a blue jean jacket adorned with patches and pins, and a strip of purple hair ran down the center of her frizzy hair.

"Ah, there you are," Mrs. Hooper said. "This is Samantha Sinclair. Would you do her a favor and help bring her up to speed on the comings and goings of the school?"

"Why me?" I asked.

"Well," Mrs. Hooper said. She stumbled for more words. "I think that's better discussed in private."

"Then I'm going to have to decline," I replied, clearing my throat.

"I'm afraid that's not an option. I was just asking to be polite."

I cocked my head and frowned. "Right, I forgot this isn't a democracy. So then, at least tell me, why, oh why, do I have this honor?"

"Because she's going to be seated next to you," Mrs. Hooper said. "And she can use a friend. After…well, you could use a new friend, too."

The whole class burst out in laughter. The teacher was trying to set me up on a playdate. How pathetic I must have seemed to them, and how little I cared about their pity.

Samantha clutched her notebook tight to her chest. It was covered with all sorts of scribblings and scratchings: pentagrams and cartoon characters and little monster doodles. As she came down the aisle toward me, she gave a slight smile, which I did not return. She needed a friend, somebody who could make her feel comfortable in her new school, but that wasn't me.

She took Katie's seat. A new person was coming in and usurping Katie's seat. The poor girl needed a friend and I recognized that, but I hated her immediately because she was not Katie, and I hated her because the moment she sat down it solidified that Katie would never come back and sit there ever again.

Samantha had ruined the one thing I liked about school.

Chapter 6

Samantha followed me out of class and down the hall. I turned to her, trying not to reveal the venom I felt for her. "So, I guess I'm your tour guide to the worst place on Earth, huh?"

"I guess so," Samantha said. "Is this place really that bad?"

I was thinking of a way to sugar coat my loathing of school when Principal Foster waved at me from down the hall. He was a bald, light-skinned black man in a perfectly tailored suit. His shoes glistened in the fluorescent lights as he stepped through the hallway.

"Ah good, Miss Aguilar," Principal Foster said with a big, fake smile. "You have found our new student."

"It was hard to miss her," I replied. "Mrs. Thomas sat her right next to me."

"Yes," Principal Foster said with a deeply uncomfortable sigh. "That was my idea. I thought it might help both of you."

"It doesn't help," I grumbled. The bell rang for class. "Now excuse me. I don't want our new student to be late."

"Of course," he said. "Keep your chin up. It does get better."

I wanted to punch him in his smug face with its condescending smile. "I doubt it."

I met Samantha outside each of her morning classes until it was time for lunch. Lunch was my least favorite part of the day because it meant socializing with humans who weren't Katie. I had no interest in seeing anyone, least of all people who were laughing with their friends while mine was dead.

"And this is another place that sucks." I pushed open the door to the cafeteria. It was pretty standard. Long picnic tables lined the room, and a disgusting lunch counter vacillated between serving sludge, muck, and gruel, depending on the day.

"So, what I've gathered is this whole place really does suck," Samantha said. "Just like my old school. Shouldn't be a problem not fitting in then."

I walked toward the back of the cafeteria. "Was that a problem at your old school? Not fitting in, I mean."

Samantha followed me. "I wouldn't call it a problem. More like a necessary survival mechanism. I'm a bit of a loner."

"Well, then it won't be much different here."

I sat down in my usual spot at the far end of the cafeteria where even the stoners and rejects didn't gather, and pulled out my brown bag lunch, which assuredly contained a chicken salad sandwich and bag of potato chips. Usually, I would have given them to Katie, or thrown them away when she was absent, but I just didn't have the energy, so I pushed them away and laid my head on the table.

"Are you going to eat that?" Samantha asked, sitting down across from me.

"I thought you were a loner. That's the one thing I liked about you."

She sighed, reaching for my chips and popping them open without asking. "I am a loner. I've been a loner in every school I've ever been to, and I've been to a lot."

"Why do you keep switching schools? Are you a delinquent or something?"

"No," she said, stuffing a handful of chips into her mouth. "Army brat. Well, Air Force brat, but that doesn't roll off the tongue so easily. I've been to eight schools in ten years, so I know a thing or two about being a loner for survival."

"And yet…you are talking to me." I sighed and put my head back on the table.

"Cuz you're like me."

"What does that mean?"

"It means I get your thing. You're alone for survival. We are the same."

I lifted my head and stared at her. "We are nothing alike."

She crunched on chips and shrugged. "Fine, but I can see somebody with the morbs from a hundred yards away."

"The morbs?"

"It's an old Victorian expression. Means being sad."

"Then yeah, I guess I have the morbs."

"Who did you lose?" she asked, taking a bite of my sandwich. "Mom, Dad, cousin?"

She'd hit a sore spot. "My best friend, okay? I mean, whatever, you're going to find out anyway."

Samantha gulped. "That was…unexpected. Did she get hit by a car or was it something you knew about?"

"Cancer. Leukemia." I buried my head in my arms on the table and tried to hold back my tears. "You ask a lot of questions."

"I like death, grief, loss, and junk. I'm fascinated by that kind of stuff. So, sue me."

I picked my head off the table again. "I'm more likely to put a restraining order out on you."

"You want me to leave, just say the word."

I did want her to leave, but I also didn't want to be alone. For some reason, no matter how much I hated her, I also wanted her around. She was the only person in my life that didn't have the smell of Katie all over them. She was the only person I could look at without seeing Katie's face, and who didn't look at me like the poor girl who'd lost her friend.

"What was her name?" Samantha asked after swallowing another bite of my sandwich.

"Katie. You would have hated her."

"Yeah? Well it's a good bet because I hate everybody, but why specifically would I hate her?"

I placed my head in my hands. "She was a ball of sunshine, all the way until the end. She was like sickeningly sunny. Even in the worst days of chemo, when she knew she wasn't going to recover, she was still…happy. I loved that about her."

"And you hated it about her too, right?"

I laughed. I hadn't laughed in weeks, and it felt foreign to me. "Yeah, I guess I kind of hated it about her, too. She never let me wallow in anything, and sometimes you want to wallow."

"Of course. Who doesn't love a good wallow?"

"Right?" I replied. "Now, I have all the time in the world for wallowing."

"Does it feel good?"

"No," I said. "It feels like nothing, or it feels horrible. One of the two, but it definitely doesn't feel good."

"Yeah, that's the worst part of it all for me. When it feels like nothing at all."

"How do you know?" I asked. "Who have you lost?"

She finished the last of the chips and licked her fingers. "My dad died last year. Airstrike in Syria. Barely any casualties on that front, but my stupid dad had to be one of them." Her eyes teared up. "It sucks. Now, I'm stuck here without him. I hated moving every couple of years, but I hate not having him around even more."

"That hole never closes completely, does it? The best you can do is shrink it down with time."

"Now you're an expert at parental death, too?"

"Kind of. My dad died when I was eleven."

"Jesus Christ," Samantha said, raising her eyebrows. "You are a walking death sentence."

I started to cry uncontrollably into my hands. She was right. It was only a joke, but she was right. I was a walking death warrant to everybody I touched and everybody I care about, and I hated her for reminding me of that. I actually could have liked Samantha, but instead I had to push her away. I couldn't risk more blood on my hands.

Chapter 7

Mom had the worst schedule. She went to school before I got home and came back after I went to bed. The only time I saw her was when she had the day off, but even then, she had projects to work on for class. She was always either trying to catch up on sleep or dragging around like a zombie trying to pretend like she wasn't exhausted.

On the lucky days, she would head into work late so we could eat together, even if she was eating her breakfast while I ate my dinner. More often than not, though, we missed each other completely. One gift Katie's death gave us was the chance to be together for a couple of days and reconnect as if we had a functional relationship. Those days were gone now.

When I walked in the door from school, I smelled chili simmering in the crock pot. I walked into the kitchen and found a note on the counter:

> *Didn't season dinner before running out.*
> *Needs chili powder for sure. Love you. Mom*

Mom didn't like a lot of spice in her chili, but I liked it hot enough to start a fire in my mouth. I scooped out a bowl and tossed a mess of cayenne pepper and adobo onto the chili. Katie would have hated it, what with her weak stomach that just got weaker over time. She could barely keep down toast by the end.

I flipped on the television, but then I caught a glimpse of Katie's house from outside my front window. The lights were off, but her mother's car was in the driveway. When Katie was alive, a bevy of doctor appointments forced Joanne to interact with the outside world, but now she only left the house to attend church.

She had taken to getting her groceries delivered since before Katie died, and took a remote job teaching Chinese students English so she could be by her daughter's side. I doubted she had eaten much since the funeral. At Katie's wake she didn't pick up so much as a cracker.

I scooped a second bowl of chili and headed across the street. Joanne didn't like spice any more than Katie did, so I didn't bother adding any additional spices into my mom's bland chili. It wasn't really about taste anyway. I just wanted to make sure she ate something, anything.

"Mrs. Allen," I said, knocking on the door with my foot. There was no movement at first, but after a few seconds, I heard footsteps walking toward the door.

The door slowly opened, and the ghost of Katie's mother stared back at me. She looked as if she hadn't bathed in days or seen the sun in even longer. At the funeral she'd made herself up to seem more together, but now, in the darkness of her own house, she looked like a zombie. She was doing a bad job of hanging on to the last vestiges of humanity.

"What is it, Anna?" she asked me with a hoarse voice. Her red, dry eyes told the story that she had just been crying for hours. The wad of balled-up tissues in her hand confirmed it.

I held up the chili. "I thought you might be hungry."

"No, I'm not," she said, trying to close the door.

I stuck my foot in the doorjamb. "Please eat. Katie would have wanted you to eat. She used to love my mother's chili."

Joanne let out a deep sigh. "She did, didn't she?"

"It's still hot," I said. "Temperature-wise, of course."

Joanne let out a soft laugh, but there was nothing behind her eyes except pain. "Come on in then. You'll catch your death out there."

We ate our chili in silence, but we didn't need to talk. It was just nice to be around somebody. Listening to her spoon hit the side of the bowl, and hearing her chew meant that I wasn't alone.

After we finished our dinner, she took our bowls into the kitchen and put them in the dishwasher. "I'll bring these to your mother tomorrow."

"No rush. It's just the two of us and we have a hundred bowls for some reason. They'll last us until doomsday."

"Yeah, it's weird, isn't it? Suddenly, I have double the bowls than I'll ever use."

I stood up. "At least you'll have to do the dishwasher half as often, I guess. Katie would have taken some solace in that. She hated the dishes."

Joanne let out the smallest breath of air, which could barely be construed as a laugh. "She really did, and she was just dreadful at it."

"She was the worst. Like, you would get something out of the drying rack, and it would be caked with food. But you know Katie, she would always claim that she washed it."

"She swore by it every time," Joanne said, shaking her head.

"Do you mind if I go up to her room?"

"Go ahead," Joanne said. "My house is your house. At least with you here it doesn't feel as lonely."

I slowly walked up the stairs. I hadn't been in Katie's room since the funeral. I just wanted to be close to her and catch her smell on the air. Maybe that was the whole reason for bringing Joanne dinner. She was the closest to Katie I would ever be again.

I pushed open the door and stepped inside the room. A cold chill whipped past me as the door slammed shut. I didn't think much of it at first. Katie's room was the coldest in the house, since it was above the garage, but I had the strange feeling something wanted me to stay inside the room.

The floorboards creaked as I moved through the room. Joanne always said she was going to fix the floor when Katie got better. She said she was going to take out the horrible shag carpet and replace it with hardwood like Katie wanted. Maybe she was trying to bribe her daughter to get better, as if that could have helped. Still, we would have tried anything, even if it meant tricking her body to get better.

Katie's room was filled with toys. Every inch was covered with Transformers, and action figures, and Hello Kitty dolls, and ceramic cats. How she got any work done was beyond me.

"I didn't." The soft voice was behind me. "I had to lay in my bed to work. Of course, I didn't have much homework by the end."

I swung around frantically in every direction. I swore I heard Katie's voice, but that was impossible. I shook my head and turned around. My mind was playing tricks on me, hearing voices on the wind.

"It's not a trick." It was Katie's voice. "And it's not the wind."

Tears filled my eyes. Why would my mind be so cruel to me? Did it want me to suffer? The air in the room felt stale in my lungs. My throat was constricted, and I knew I needed to leave. I was going to hyperventilate. I clawed at my throat, trying to breathe again. I opened the door to her room and ran outside into the hall, leaping down the stairs and out the door without saying goodbye to Joanne.

Tears filled my eyes as I ran across the street. I ran up to my room, locking the door behind me. In my own bed, I could breathe again, and slowly everything went back to normal. Or as normal as I could ever expect, given that my best friend was dead.

Chapter 8

I heard Katie's voice in my head all night. I tossed and turned, trying to find a place where she wasn't speaking to me. It turned out to be an impossible task. All night, she kept trying to get my attention, but I had to ignore her voice.

She wasn't real. She wasn't talking to me. Katie was dead.

The next morning, I forced Mom to drive me to the cemetery before school. All she wanted to do was sleep, but I needed to be reminded that Katie was still buried six feet into the ground.

"Is there anything I can do?" my mom asked after standing over Katie's grave for ten minutes.

The soil was still fresh and the flowers we placed on the headstone hadn't wilted yet. It was all so new still. I couldn't tell Mom the truth about why we were there. I couldn't tell her that I was going crazy.

"You're not crazy," Katie's voice whispered in my ear. "You're not crazy."

I wanted to believe her, but that's the kind of thing a crazy person would believe. I certainly didn't think I was losing my mind, but then nobody ever thought they were crazy. They thought they were the sanest person in the world. That didn't change the fact that I was hearing Katie's voice even though she was dead. I was standing over her grave, watching the wind blow dirt off the top of it.

"Can we go?" my mom said. "I don't want to cheapen your grief, but I just worked a long shift and I need to sleep, kiddo."

"Fine." I nodded.

Walking away from her grave, I swore I saw a haunting blue light under the willow tree that hung down over Katie's grave. That's when I knew I was going crazy. Not only was I hearing Katie, now I was seeing her, too.

Crazy people still had to go to school, though. I had already missed enough days throughout the year sitting by Katie's bedside, and I had a slew of work I'd fallen behind on after her funeral. My teachers were all very understanding, but not understanding enough to just give me an A without doing the work. I needed top marks if I wanted to be valedictorian.

"You look horrible," Samantha said, sitting down next to me. I hadn't gotten over a usurper in Katie's seat. I knew Samantha wasn't intentionally slapping my best friend in the face by sitting next to me, but just the fact that she existed was enough to cut the wound of Katie's death even deeper.

"So do you."

She didn't actually look horrible. She had tied her frizzy, brown hair into big, bushy pig tails, and they looked quite cute with the green and black flannel that she'd tied up at the waist.

"I got up at five am to get ready for today," she said. "So, I don't believe you. You, on the other hand, look like you haven't slept in days."

She was right. I hadn't slept in days. Not really. Every day since Katie's death I'd slept worse and worse, and I wasn't even sure whether I'd slept at all the night before.

I hadn't slept well in the months leading up to Katie's death, either. Every single day, I thought I would wake up and she would be gone, and then one day I was right. If I hadn't slept so long the night of her death, maybe I could have seen Katie one last time. Maybe I would have told her one last time that I loved her.

"Hello?" Samantha said. I realized I had been locked in a daze for several minutes without answering her.

Mercifully, Mrs. Thomas spoke up before I had to answer Samantha. "All right, class. Now, on to today's lesson."

She wasn't much of an orator, but I still paid close attention. Even in the most boring lectures I could lock in on taking notes. I used to take notes for Katie and was diligent about them. I wasn't much of a student before she got sick, but I learned how to learn for her, so that I could recite everything to her.

Before I knew it, the bell rang, and class was over. Samantha had been following me from class to class, and I had to get out of there before she tracked me down. I felt slightly bad leaving her to fend for herself, but I just couldn't deal with her. Not today.

Luckily, I knew the hiding places in school like the back of my hand, and I used them whenever I needed to get away from the crowd. My favorite was the bathroom next to the janitor's closet on the second floor.

It was inconvenient and dark. Nobody went there, not even to smoke or ditch, because it was supposed to be only used by teachers. Of course, even teachers didn't use it because it was out of the way from their classrooms. So, I usually had it to myself, except when Katie joined me. I guess I would have it to myself forever now.

"This always was your favorite place," Katie's voice whispered to me.

"Get out of my head," I said, pacing back and forth. "What do you want from me? Isn't it enough that I'm racked with guilt and pain? Do you have to drive me crazy, too?"

"I'm not trying to drive you crazy," Katie replied. "I'm here because I need your help. Because the world needs your help."

I scoffed. "Oh, does it? That's pretty convenient."

"It's not convenient. It sucks, but that doesn't change the fact that I need your help."

"To do what?"

"Save the world," Katie said. "I thought we'd been over this already."

"Oh, is that all? Nobody would come to me to save the world, Katie. You know that, and I know that. You wouldn't even be here if you knew me at all."

"That's not true," she said. "You're the perfect person to help me. You're kind, and wise, and brave, and…"

I paced across the tile floor. "And a mess. None of this holds up to scrutiny, Katie. None of it."

"Life doesn't hold up to scrutiny, Anna Banana."

I pressed my hands to my ears. "I hate that name."

"Not when I say it, you don't."

I slammed my hands against the counter. "This sucks. How am I supposed to get over you if I can't get you out of my head?"

"How do you think I feel?" Katie said. "I'm dead, and my friend doesn't believe I'm really here. If this sucks for you, think of how much it must suck for me."

"I do think about that," I said. "I think about that all the time. It's almost all I think about."

From under the only stall in the room, a blue light began to show. I caught it in the mirror, throbbing dimly at first, but it began to fill the room with light. I waited for it to explode out of the stall, but it didn't. Instead, it pushed through the metal door and floated in front of me.

I couldn't believe my eyes. It looked like Katie. Not the Katie from the last days of her sickness, but the Katie that was full of life. The one with long hair and chubby cheeks, who ran and played with me like she didn't have a care in the world, back when we didn't have a care in the world.

"I thought this would be easier for you," she said, "but we don't have much time."

My mind fritzed out, and my eyes went black. It was too much for my brain to handle. I fell onto the floor and my mind drifted away.

A few minutes later, I woke up, and Katie was gone. The bell rang, and I pushed myself off the floor and ran to class. I was going to need help to get over Katie appearing before me. Professional help.

Chapter 9

I had been going to therapy on and off since my father died, but after Katie was diagnosed with cancer, I went all the time. I thought I would hate it, but I honestly loved therapy. It's the only place in the whole world where I could talk about my fears and problems without somebody judging me. I couldn't talk about Katie with Mom or Joanne, because I didn't want to make them depressed or anything. They had enough on their plates, and I didn't need to pile on any more.

Therapy was my sanctuary, which was why it was so disappointing that Katie's ghost showed up during my appointment. I knew it wasn't actually her, but it made it hard to concentrate on the doctor when Katie was staring at me in her fake, glowing, blue body.

"I'm sorry about your friend, Anna," Doctor Rachel said after we'd sat in silence for a long time. I didn't like calling doctors by their first names, but if it helped her feel more relatable, I was willing to do it for her, since in every other way she was amazing.

She was younger than any other doctor I had ever met. She didn't seem older than thirty, though I never asked how old she was. That would be impolite. All I cared about was that I felt safe around her. I don't think I would have felt safe around an old, stuffy doctor, but Doctor Rachel had bookcases accented with Power Rangers and Ninja Turtles, which made her all right in my book.

"Thank you," I said. "It's been…hard."

"I can imagine," she said. "I mean, I can only imagine. It's not like anything like that has ever happened to me."

What I liked most about Doctor Rachel was that she didn't talk down to me. She didn't sugar coat things or pretend to have all the answers. She just wanted to help, even if it was messy.

"It sucks," I said, my eyes ping ponging back and forth between Doctor Rachel and the ghost of Katie in the corner of the room.

"You seem distracted," Doctor Rachel said, watching me.

I rubbed my eyes with my hands. "I—I am. Honestly. Can I ask you something, and have you not think I should be committed afterwards?"

Doctor Rachel tilted her head. "Well, I can't guarantee that. I mean, I can try to be understanding, but if you tell me you're going to hurt yourself—"

I held up my hands emphatically. "Oh no, nothing like that. It's just…if somebody was to hear the voice of their dead friend in their head, does that make them crazy?"

"This is my real voice!" Katie said, indignant. "I'm right here, in front of you. Why are you being so stubborn, Banana!"

"I'm being stubborn because you're not real," I mumbled.

"Excuse me?" Doctor Rachel asked.

"Nothing."

Doctor Rachel furrowed her brow. "Were you speaking to Katie, just now?"

"M—maybe…?" I said, hesitantly. "That makes me crazy, right? I mean, that has to make me crazy."

"I don't think you're crazy," Doctor Rachel said. Her voice was even-toned. "I think you've gone through a great trauma, and your mind can do a lot to get you to reconcile a loss like you've had. Tell me, how are you sleeping?"

"I'm not," I said. "I mean, not well, at least."

"Well, lack of sleep can bring on hallucinations."

"I'm not a hallucination!" Katie groaned, throwing up her hands. "Please, Anna, listen to me."

But I didn't listen to her. I couldn't. It was bad enough that I was hearing Katie's voice in my head. It was worse to listen to it, and act on it.

"So, you're saying I need a good night's sleep? That seems kind of cheap, don't you think? You don't think I need to be pumped full of pills, or taken to the looney bin?"

"No, I don't, and I didn't say that. I do think you need a good night's sleep, but I also think you need time. Katie just died, and you have to deal with that pain. Grief is a process that takes time. This is going to sound trite, but do you know the five stages of grief?"

"Denial, depression, binge eating, sitting alone in the dark, and then acceptance. They told me about it when my father died."

I was a wreck after my father's death, but even in the worst throes of my grief, I never heard the man in my head, or saw the ghost of him around me.

"That's because I'm not a hallucination," Katie said. "I'm real. I mean, I'm a ghost, but I'm real."

"Stop it," I grumbled. "Go away."

Katie hovered toward me. "Is that what you want, Banana? Really? Do you really want me to go away?"

"No," I replied. "It's just…" I stopped myself. I couldn't keep talking to an imaginary ghost. Even for a sleep deprived girl, I could tell by Doctor Rachel's eyes that it wasn't normal. "I'm sorry."

"You don't have to apologize to me," Doctor Rachel said. "Grief is a process."

I wasn't apologizing to her. I was apologizing to Katie, but I couldn't tell the doctor that, so I just smiled. "Thanks for understanding."

Chapter 10

I didn't talk the whole way home from therapy, which made Mom think I was mad at her. I had to stay silent though, because the minute I spoke, Katie was in my ear trying to talk to me, and I couldn't have my mother thinking I was crazy. It was one thing to talk openly about my hallucinations with Doctor Rachel. Her office was a safe space.

That didn't make us friends, of course, because if we became friends then I would be opening her up for the curse of Anna. The one that left everybody I loved dead or wounded.

"You're not cursed," Katie said from the back seat. "You've just been unlucky up 'til now, but maybe that means you're going to be super lucky in the future. Did you ever think of that?"

I hadn't thought of that, but I wasn't about to start now. After all, Katie was just a figment of my imagination trying to make me feel better. Keeping everybody at a distance allowed me to live with myself. It allowed me to know that nobody else would be hurt because of me.

"I have tomorrow off, you know," Mom said as she pulled into the driveway. "I was thinking that maybe we could go to the zoo. I know you and Katie liked that. What do you think?"

We did like that, especially the bat enclosure. It was a weird thing to like, and more than a little creepy, but Katie liked being scared. You wouldn't think that about her, with how nice and sweet she was, but she loved being scared. We would stay up all night sometimes watching movies like *Friday the 13th* and *Hereditary*.

"Maybe," I said. "Probably not though. I kind of just want to veg."

I didn't like being scared, which made being friends with Katie very hard, especially at night. I would do anything for just one day where I could watch scary movies with her again.

"Would that make you happy?" Katie asked as I got out of the car. "I will watch all the scary movies with you if you just listen to me."

I didn't say anything until I got into my room, but the minute I closed the door I threw down my coat and wheeled on her.

"What?" I asked. "What kind of crazy thing do you want me to do, Katie? Oh wait, it doesn't matter, because you're not real."

"I am real," Katie said.

"Then why can nobody else see you?"

"I don't know," Katie replied coolly. "It's not like I want anybody to see me except for you, so I didn't ask any questions about it. I figured if anybody would understand that, it would be you."

"Well, I don't understand," I said, plopping down on the bed. "Or I guess, I do understand. I understand that I'm crazy. Maybe if I just sleep this will all be over. Maybe I'm just delusional from lack of sleep."

Katie hovered into my line of sight. "That won't make me go away, Anna. I need your help."

"Go find somebody else to bother then."

"I don't want to find somebody else. I want you to help me. I want you to believe me."

I flung my hands into the air, exasperated. "How can I believe you, Katie? You're dead. I know you're dead. If I believe you, I have to believe that ghosts are real, and that's nonsense."

"It's not nonsense," Katie replied. "Everybody eventually becomes a ghost. Your dad is a ghost."

"Watch it," I said. "Don't say another word about my father."

"Or what?" Katie said with a snicker. "You'll hurt me?"

"No," I said. "I'll hurt myself. If you really are Katie, you'll never let me do that to myself."

"Fine," she said. "You always were stubborn. Isn't there anything I can do to convince you?"

"Sure. Tell me something I don't know. Anything."

"You know everything about me," Katie said. "Literally everything."

"Well, then I guess there's nothing you can do."

Katie sighed. "There is one thing, but I don't think I should tell you. It might hurt you, and I don't want to hurt you."

I folded my arms across my chest. "Then I guess we're done here. Go haunt somebody else."

There was a long silence. For a moment, I thought she might be gone, but when I tilted my head up, she was hovering over the corner of my bed.

"I loved you," she said, softly.

"I loved you, too," I replied. "That's not news."

"No," Katie said, turning to me. "I loved you loved you."

"Don't lie to me," I replied. "That's not fair. You're in my brain. You know how I felt about you, and…that's not fair to lie to me; to use my own feelings against me."

"I'm not lying," Katie replied. "I have proof. Or more like, there's proof in my room."

"You're right. I don't believe you."

"You don't have to believe me. Just get up and walk across the street, and I'll show you where the proof is."

I sat up in bed. "Fine."

I pushed myself off the bed and rushed to the door. I had never been angrier in my whole life, but even in my anger, a little piece of me hoped it was true. It was just my brain acting out my deepest desire. I had always loved Katie, not as a sister, but as so much more. I never told her, and that was my biggest regret.

Chapter 11

She'd better not be lying to me. She'd better not be lying to me. She'd better not be lying to me.

I couldn't believe I was entertaining the thought that a ghost was telling me the truth as I marched across the street to Joanne's house.

"I'm not lying to you," Katie said as I knocked on the door.

I shook my head. "No, you aren't lying to me. My subconscious is lying to me, because my subconscious is cruel."

Joanne swung the door open. She looked around before looking at me. "Who are you talking to?"

"Nobody," I said, turning my eyes to her. "Can I come in?"

"Of course." Joanne held open the door.

"Where am I going?" I whispered into the ether.

"Upstairs. Into my room."

"Do you mind if I go upstairs again?" I asked. "I think I left something up there yesterday."

"You don't need a reason, dear," Joanne said. "You can come and go as you please."

"Thanks."

I marched up the stairs, fully aware that I had now crossed over from crazy to bonkers. I wasn't just hearing the voice in my head, I was following its commands. It was some John Wayne Gacy level stuff.

"As long as you don't put on a clown costume, I think you'll be fine," Katie said as I turned the corner toward her room.

"If you're not in my head, how come you can hear my thoughts?"

"I don't know," she said. "I'd be lying if I said I understood how this ghost thing worked, honestly. It's not like there's a spirit guide to show you how to be a ghost. You just kind of wing it."

"There's not? That must make it hard." I shook my head again. "I can't believe I'm talking to myself."

"You're not," Katie replied. "And no, there isn't. You're on your own. Even if you find a ghost…never mind."

"What is it?" I asked, walking up the steps.

"It's nothing," she said. "Just…let me prove I'm real to you first."

"Good luck." I swung open the door to her room. "What now?"

Katie pointed to the bed. "Under the mattress."

"A little cliché, isn't it?"

"Well, it's not like I had the energy to do much else or go many other places. My bed was my sanctuary."

I pushed up the mattress. Sure enough, wedged in under the sheets was a marbled notebook with the words KEEP OUT across the front.

"Don't worry about the warning," Katie said. "That's just when I was alive."

"What if your mom found it?" I said. "I mean…after."

"I didn't think much about it," Katie said. "I just needed a place that I could tell the truth. There's no way you knew about this notebook."

"I don't know. I guess you could have talked about it and I forgot. It seeped into my subconscious or something."

"Trust me. I would NEVER have told you about this journal. Not ever."

I opened the notebook. Scribbled across the front page a hundred times was the name "Katherine Eugenia Aguilar." The first three pages were nothing but her first name and my last name written together.

"What is this?" I asked.

"I was practicing, for in case we got married, and I was going to change my name." She hid herself behind her hands. "Man, this is so embarrassing."

I flipped through the pages. Every one of them was filled with her inner most thoughts and feelings. On the tenth page, for instance, she wrote:

> *Anna came over today. I vomited in front of her. It was the most embarrassed I've ever been in my entire life.*

"Why would you be embarrassed about that?" I asked, looking up from the notebook and catching Katie's eyes.

"Cuz I didn't want you to see me like that. I mean have you ever had the flu so bad you were sweaty and yucky and throwing up?"

"Yeah, you know I have, back in eighth grade."

"And did you want your crush to see you all like that, gross and ugly?"

"No," I said, closing the notebook. "But they did anyway."

"What are you talking about? The only one that saw you was me. You wouldn't even let your mom in—" Katie paused. "Oh."

"Yeah," I said. "I have a confession of my own. Since we're being honest."

"What is it?" Katie asked. Her voice was breathy, like she was nervous.

"I love you, too."

"Really?" she smiled, floating higher into the air. Her blue glow shined brighter as she rose toward the ceiling.

"Really," I said. "I've never loved anybody more in my entire life."

"Wow." Katie smiled sadly. "I guess we should have said something when I was alive."

I nodded. "I guess so."

Katie settled down onto the ground. "So, do you believe me now?"

"How can I not?" I said. "I mean, if you had ever said anything about this I would have been over the moon. I don't know how I believe you, but I do."

"It's about time," Katie said. "Now, we have work to do."

I looked up. "What kind of work?"

"We have to save the world."

I stood up and walked toward the door. "Let's go save the world then, I guess."

"Wait," Katie said. "Put down the notebook."

"Oh, come on," I said, holding it to my chest. "Can't I just read through it a little bit more?"

"No," Katie said. "Put it back, and never look at it again."

I sighed and stuffed the book back under the bed. "Fine, but I'm not happy about it."

"Well, I'm dead, and I'm not happy about that either. We can't get what we want, can we?"

"I guess not. Okay. I'm putting it back, but, if I do that, you have to do something for me."

"What?"

I cleared my throat. "Stay out of my head."

"Oh, but I like it in there."

"I'm serious. I don't like you hearing my thoughts any more than you like me reading yours."

"All right," Katie said, nodding her head. "You have a deal. I don't like it."

I looked back to her bed, where the diary stuffed with secrets was hidden. "That makes two of us."

"Come with me," Katie said with a smile, and she floated out of the room. I didn't know where she was going, but I knew I would follow her to the ends of the Earth.

Chapter 12

"Where are we going?" I asked as Katie led me down our street.

She glanced over her shoulder. "I have something to show you."

I followed behind her until she reached the edge of the woods at the end of our street. We used to play in those woods all the time. There were frogs to catch, leaf piles to jump in, and one summer my father even built us a tire swing that swung out over the creek running through the middle of the woods.

"It's in here," Katie said. "Don't be scared."

"I'm not scared," I said. "I'm with you."

I knew I might be out of my mind to believe I was following a ghost, but she had told me something I didn't know before. That meant she couldn't be a hallucination of my own mind. She told me that she loved me, really loved me. My heart started to flutter thinking how much I loved her, too.

"Why didn't you tell me?" I asked, walking through the woods.

"Why didn't you tell me?" Katie replied.

"You were dealing with a lot, and I didn't want to add something else to your plate. Besides, if you were going to reject me, I didn't want it to get awkward."

"What made you think I would reject you?"

I stepped over a log, only able to see it in the dark because of Katie's glowing blue aura. "I don't know. I mean, it's hard enough being a human when you like boys, and stuff. Liking girls, and your best friend on top of it. That's extra levels of awkward."

Katie turned back to me. "I wish you had told me."

"Well, yeah. I wish I did, too, knowing what I know now. Why didn't you tell me?"

Katie stopped and hovered in place. "I didn't want to know the truth. If you didn't like me, then I might have lost my best friend. And if you did, well, I didn't want you to have to deal with a dead girlfriend. It's hard enough dealing with a dead friend."

"But we would have had those few months together. That would have made it all worth it."

"Maybe, but now, you would have to deal with losing me, not just friend me, but…I didn't want you to have to go through that."

I walked toward Katie's floating ghost. "That's so stupid."

She shrugged. "Maybe. It's my reasoning though, stupid or not."

I wanted to touch her, to hug her, but when I reached my arm out, my hand fell right through her. She wasn't wrong. Knowing that she had loved me made it feel like I had lost her all over again; harder still was knowing that we could have been together, and we were too scared to say the words to each other.

"Yeah," Katie said, watching me return my hand to my side. "We can't, like, touch. That makes this even more awkward. I think we should just move on from what we said to each other and figure out how to save the world."

"So just not talk about it?" I asked.

"At least not right now," Katie said, floating forward through the woods again.

"Fair enough. This is all really weird, and I don't know if I can handle being in love with a ghost right now. I can barely handle losing my best friend. Let's focus on why you're here then. Why are you here?"

"I'm here to save your world."

"Yes, you've said that…can you be a little more specific?"

"It's a little complicated, but I'll try. There is a rift between your world and mine. A barrier that separates the living and the dead. We call that the Dark Place."

"Because it's dark?"

Katie nodded. "It's so dark we can barely see the light from other ghosts in the darkness."

"And something is wrong with it?"

"Yes," Katie nodded. "The partition that separates Earth from the Dark Place has punctured, and now has a hole in it where one world bleeds into the other. If we don't close it back up, then the tear will continue to grow, and it will envelop all of you along with it, destroying Earth."

"That sounds pretty bad."

"It's worse than that," Katie said. "It's the end of your world."

I walked into a clearing where Katie and I used to play volleyball. Except there was no volleyball in the woods that night. Instead, there was a giant black hole in the sky. Blue fire shot out of it as ghosts flooded out into the world.

"Why isn't the army, or NASA out here quarantining the area?"

"You watch too many movies," Katie said. "Nobody else can see it but you, just like nobody can see me but you."

"Seems stupid. I feel like the FBI would be pretty interested in this if they could see it. They probably have some interdimensional laser already in development to close that thing right up."

"Yeah, maybe they could help, but then I would become a science experiment. I mean, a real live ghost would keep them funded for decades, and I would rather not be poked and prodded for their experiments."

"Now who's seen too many movies, ET?"

Katie chuckled. "I think we can fix it without them."

"Fix it? You think we're going to fix this by ourselves?"

"We might have to bring in a little help, but yes. I do. I have faith in us."

"I think your faith is a little misplaced. That thing is huge."

"It was half this size when I came out of it to find you. It's growing every day."

I stared at the giant hole. "What do we do?"

"No idea," Katie replied. "This is bad, Anna, and I don't know the first thing about fixing it."

"Wow."

"What?"

"Well, it seemed as though you had a plan, with all the grandstanding about not needing the FBI and all."

"I don't have a plan, but I wasn't lying when I said that I believe in us."

"It's okay," I said. "It's okay. We'll figure it out."

I only wished I believed myself, but that wasn't important. What was important was saying it confidently enough that Katie felt my confidence in her. We could figure anything out together.

Chapter 13

We searched the internet for the rest of the night, but we couldn't come up with anything about how to repair a rift to the Dark Place. We found some cool lyrics from death metal songs, and a couple very poorly categorized recipes, but when the sun rose, we were no closer to finding out how to fix the hole Katie showed me in the woods.

"Maybe somebody else will find it," I said, falling back exhausted on my desk chair. "Can't somebody else figure this out?"

"Who else even knows about the woods, Banana? We're the only kids left on this street that didn't move away or go to college."

"Maybe one of the other ghosts will figure it out."

"I wouldn't count on it," Katie replied. "Something happens to you when you're in there too long."

"What happens?" I asked.

"I don't know, but every time I tried to talk to a ghost, they just stared at me blankly. You lose your shape in there, and your form. Some of the ghosts I saw were just puddles, and others were just rectangles. You stop remembering people, too. I found my dad in there. He didn't…he didn't remember my name. You just fall apart. I don't know how to describe it better than…well, you know Slimer?"

"From *Ghostbusters*?"

"He used to be a human at some point, but then he became just a mass of ooze, right?"

"Yeah, I guess that's what happened. I mean, now that I think about it, Slimer must have been a human at some point, or at least something besides gelatinous ooze."

"Well, it's like that. Maybe they were people at some point, but they aren't anymore. I doubt they even remember who they were. I only remembered because I just died, but even after a couple of days I started to forget everything I once knew. I started to forget you, my mom, and…everything."

"Sounds horrible."

"You would think, except that it was freeing in a way. I felt lighter, untethered. It was horrible and wonderful all at once."

"I don't see how it would be wonderful to forget everything you once knew."

Katie turned away from me. "Let's hope you don't have to experience it for a long time."

I turned back to the computer. It wasn't that there weren't websites talking about repairing rifts in time and space. There were thousands of them. It's just that none of them were reliable, and they all contradicted each other. Fred-meat-popsicle.com gave one set of instructions and then Zelda_witch.net said the exact opposite thing. It's not like there was a widely recognized site related to the afterlife we could just cross reference. Most of it was garbage, and the rest of it was washed out by the deluge of useless information.

"Wait," I said as the sun crept into my window. "What about church?"

"What about church?" Katie replied.

"Think about it. They say they're professional exorcists and deal with death. Like, if anybody would know about the afterlife they would, right?"

"Sure, maybe. But there are like a million religions out there. How are you going to pick which one to believe?"

"Well, we live in a small town, and there's only a couple churches, so I say we start with what we know and work out from there."

"Did my mother have Father Thomas do my service?"

I shook my head. "You didn't want a religious service. She fought every instinct, but she didn't ask the Father to your service. It nearly killed her, but she respected your wishes."

"Good. Religion is dumb. Lot of good any of it did me. I saw every priest and faith healer in the world, and none of them helped me."

"Your mom still goes to mass, though. It's about the only time she leaves the house."

"I guess it's as good a place as any to start. At the very least, it's something to check off the list of things we've tried."

Joanne had attended seven o' clock mass every night for months. She wasn't very spiritual before Katie was diagnosed, but as the odds around her child's survival dimmed, her devotion to God increased. She wasn't the first one and she wouldn't be the last.

"I'm surprised you wanted to come with me," Joanne said as we drove to church together. "I know this isn't your thing. It wasn't Katie's thing, either. I just had to pray harder for all of us."

"Well," I replied. "I am still trying to make sense of it all, and I figured church was as good a place as any to do that."

"It really is," Joanne said. "I don't know where I would be now without the church to guide me."

Katie snickered from the back seat. She always thought it was stupid that her mother found religion, and the more devoted her mom became, the stupider Katie found it. I tried not to laugh along with her. After all, I was the only person who could see her.

I didn't know why Katie acted like she was sitting in the back seat when she was clearly floating along with us. Perhaps it was because she wanted to feel normal for a second, even though nothing about our situation was normal in the slightest.

The Church of St. Mark rested on a large plot of land in the middle of town. The church loomed large over the surrounding acreage and was equal parts welcoming and ominous, in the way that only Catholics could be.

Father Thomas smiled at us when he saw us enter the church. "Joanne, so nice to see you tonight, and you brought a friend along."

"Yes," Joanne said. "This is Anna Aguilar. You may remember her from the funeral."

"Yes," Father Thomas said, stretching out his hand toward me. "Your face does look familiar. Please, come in."

"Thank you, Father. I was hoping you might answer some questions for me."

The church bell rang, and Father Thomas looked up at the clock above the vestibule. "I'm afraid I'm a little busy right now, but if you stay until after the service, I'll be happy to answer any of your questions."

"Do you mind, Joanne?" I asked.

She smiled at me. "Of course not. Anything I can do to help bring Jesus into your heart is okay by me."

I couldn't bring myself to tell her that I didn't really care about that, nor explain my true purpose, so I just politely nodded. "Thank you."

"I thought you said that Father Thomas wasn't at my funeral?" Katie said to me as I took a seat in one of the pews.

I turned to her and whispered. "He was there, but he didn't preside over it. She couldn't prevent him from coming."

"Oh," Katie said. "I guess that's fair."

Chapter 14

The church service ran long. Mercilessly long. Father Thomas sure liked to hear himself talk, and he forced everybody in the congregation to suffer through his words as well.

"This is so boring," Katie said to me halfway through the homily. "Does he know how boring he is?"

She was trying to get me to laugh, but I couldn't. Father Thomas was going on and on about the horribleness of abortion, and cracking a smile wasn't something I could do without offending everybody around me, especially Joanne.

When I wouldn't reply to her, Katie floated up to the lectern and made faces behind Father Thomas's body. One advantage of being dead seemed to be that nobody could see you goof off, which meant you could do anything you wanted.

"I'll be right back," I whispered to Joanne before stepping out of the pew. I barely made it into the bathroom before I burst out laughing.

"Finally!" Katie said, floating into the bathroom after me. "That took forever."

"What are you doing in here?" I shrieked. "You can't be in here."

"Relax," Katie said. "It's not like we've never hid in a bathroom together before."

"Yeah, but that was different."

"Different how?"

"Well, for one, you weren't a ghost, and for two, you hadn't professed your love for me yet."

"So, if I was alive, cancer ridden, and hiding my feelings for you, we could share a bathroom no problem?"

"I guess. I mean, I don't know. I just know that it doesn't feel right."

"None of this feels right," Katie replied. "I'm not supposed to be dead. I wasn't supposed to get cancer. I'm not supposed to be a ghost, and yet, here we are."

"Okay," I said. "Now I really do have to pee."

"So pee."

"I can't with you floating there. Wait outside."

"This is stupid," Katie said, floating out through the wall. "But whatever."

When I was done in the bathroom, I washed my hands and met Katie in the vestibule. Father Thomas had finally ended his sermon, and the congregation was lining up for communion. I was a heathen who hadn't confessed her sins in years, so I didn't qualify to receive the blood of Christ. Instead, I decided to wait in the foyer until mass was dismissed.

Joanne walked up to me with a worried look. "Where were you?"

"Sorry," I replied. "I had to use the bathroom, and then I just decided to wait up here."

"You missed communion."

"I haven't confessed in years, Joanne. I don't think I qualify."

Joanne waved at the priest. "Well, you can do it now, and then join me tomorrow."

"No offense, Joanne, but I don't think that's going to happen."

"If you don't want a confession, then why do you need to talk to the priest?"

I smiled. "I'm sorry Joanne, but I'm afraid that's between me and the Lord."

I waited for the rest of the congregation to file outside, and when we were alone, Father Thomas walked me to his confessional in the corner of the church. It wasn't a wooden box like I had seen in the movies. It was just a room, where we sat on either side of a plain wooden coffee table, like we were having tea.

"What sins do you have to confess, my dear?"

"Whoa," I said. "I don't have sins to confess, but if I did, shouldn't we be in one of those big wooden rooms with the little sliding grate?"

"I'm afraid we don't do that here."

I shrugged. "I just thought that was the way Catholics did things."

"Yes, I'm afraid it's a common misperception. Other churches have the 'confessional' as you are describing it, but we do not."

"Weird," Katie said. She had floated in during Father Thomas's explanation. "This is where I had my first confession."

Father Thomas didn't hear any of that because he couldn't see Katie. Instead, he sat still with a pleasant look on his face while my eyes darted between him and Katie. "If you aren't here for confession, why are you here, Anna?"

"I need to ask you about ghosts."

Father Thomas sighed. "Not again. Are you another of those ghost catchers? What is it about people and ghosts these days? Don't tell me you're putting on a paranormal show, too."

"No," I said, shaking my head. "My friend just died, as you know, and I was wondering if there was any way to contact her."

Katie giggled as the priest gave me a concerned look. It was like I'd told him I was going to murder someone. "Anna, once a person moves on, they are no longer in our care. They are in the hands of the Lord."

"So, is that on another plane of existence?"

"In a way, sure. The Lord is neither temporal or corporeal, and neither are our souls."

"Is that what ghosts would be, if they existed? Souls, do you think?"

"I'm not sure."

"Can you humor me, Father? I'm having a tough time with Katie's death. This is helping."

"Very well," Father Thomas said with a sigh. "I suppose, in a way, if ghosts existed, they would be the soul of a human struggling to get to the Lord."

"He's just a jerk," Katie said. "There's no God. At least, none that I saw. Just a lot of darkness, and other ghosts turning into blobs of jelly."

"I can tell by your eyes that you have something you want to ask me, but you are, as they say, beating around the bush about it."

I lowered my head. "All right. I'll come out with it. Do you know how to heal a rift between the living and the dead?"

"I don't understand," Father Thomas replied, squinting and giving a shake of his head.

"Say there was a tear in the fabric of reality that separated living and dead people. Is there any way to patch the fabric—like, sew it up, so it didn't get any bigger?"

"My dear," Father Thomas said after clearing his throat. "I have been a priest for twenty years, and in seminary for several more, and I have never heard something so fantastical in all my life."

I sighed. "Of course you haven't. Another dead end."

"Well, at least we knocked it off the list," Katie said.

"And wasted an evening in the process," I muttered.

"Excuse me?" The priest gave me another worried look.

I stood up. "Nothing, Father. Thank you for your time."

Chapter 15

I waited at the bus stop the next morning in the cold, alone. Well, not really alone. Katie hovered next to me, her warm, blue glow lighting the dim morning.

"You really shouldn't be going to school today," she said. "We have way too much to do."

"I know that you never really valued school, but I do."

"It's not that I didn't value it. It's just that I knew I wouldn't need it. I mean, either I was going to die, or I would be able to make up the work. They're not going to fail a girl with cancer, now are they?"

"We weren't all born so lucky as to get cancer." I regretted the words the moment I said them. "I'm sorry. That was—"

"No, it's fine. I'm dead. I mean what do I care, right? But it was just luck that I got it, when you think about it. Stupid, dumb luck, but luck all the same. And I was going to use that crappy luck to give me as many boosts as possible."

"Like your 'Make a Wish.'"

Katie laughed. "I mean, who doesn't want to meet John Cena?"

"Seems like everybody does. He's visited more sick kids than anyone I hear."

"By a wide margin, and for good reason. Dude is awesome. He benched pressed me with one arm."

"Yeah, but you were like, seventy pounds by then."

"You couldn't bench press me as a ghost with both arms."

I was laughing now, too. "That's true. Give me a year to train I probably still couldn't do it."

I wondered what would happen if somebody came around the corner and saw me talking to the air. Would they think I was talking to myself? Would they think I'd lost it? Would they think I was crazy? They probably thought all those things already, honestly, and I was oddly okay with that.

Finally, good old Bus 523 came to pick me up. By then the conversation was completely one-sided. Katie talked to me, but I didn't talk back. I didn't need everyone thinking I'd lost my mind. I think she enjoyed having my undivided attention. We usually shared the spotlight equally, but when I was riding to school, or with other people, she knew she could monopolize the conversation.

I appreciated that she didn't sneak into my head and try to read my thoughts. I loved Katie, but there were some things that were too personal for her to know, and I needed some place that was sacred.

By the time we got to school, even Katie was tired of talking, and she never got tired of talking. Even on her worst days, she would go on and on for hours, as I laid at her bedside stroking her hair. She even mumbled in her sleep.

"I still don't like this place," Katie said as we got off the bus. "In fact, I think I hate it."

That didn't stop her from following me into school like a lost puppy dog. She hadn't been to school since October, and it was March now. She missed half of last year because of the cancer treatments, and I wonder if she hated school because she never got to attend or because school was boring and tedious.

Katie had been a cheerleader and soccer star. Everybody loved her, and it was easy to think that would continue forever…until it didn't. She was already talking about playing soccer at Yale, even. And then she collapsed.

At the hospital, she told me she'd been sick for a while, but she still tried to play it off. She figured she was just training too hard, and she was going to lay off after football season. But she'd been standing there, right in the middle of the school sigil—a big, blue bear—and then she'd just collapsed.

We passed over the same emblem now that she was a ghost, and her eyes lingered on it for a moment. I stopped and waited for her until the flood of bus riders rolled in and bowled right through Katie, as if they didn't even see her. Of course, that was because nobody could see her.

The shock of a group of people passing through her woke Katie out of her funk and she floated toward me to catch up. "I hate this place."

"It's okay," I mumbled under my breath, trying to stop my lips from moving so nobody could see me talking to the air.

"I know," she replied, but it wasn't really okay. She had come back to the place where it had all started to go downhill for her. The paramedics placed her on a stretcher on that spot and brought her to the hospital where she was tested for three days, and two weeks later she was diagnosed with stage three leukemia. Without a bone marrow donor, it escalated to stage four, and when chemo and radiation did nothing to stop the growth, she was labeled terminal.

Eighteen months after she fell on top of that stupid emblem of a blue bear, Katie was dead. I would hate this place too if it brought back such bad memories.

"Can I ask you something?" Katie said as I walked to class. I nodded. "Can I please read your thoughts, at least when we're with other people? This is torture, and so boring. Plus, what if you say something I need to hear?"

"Okay," I whispered as I sat down in my seat in Mrs. Hooper's class.

"Thank you!" Katie said, smiling. She took a seat in her old chair next to mine.

"Just when we're with people, though," I thought to her, "and you have to ask first."

"Deal," Katie said, turning toward the front as if she was getting ready for the lecture.

Katie was sitting there, hovering over her seat, when Samantha walked briskly into the classroom. She pushed up her glasses as she turned down the aisle next to me.

"Get up," I thought to Katie. She was staring off into space and apparently didn't hear me, or anything, until Samantha slammed her books down and slid into the seat right on top of Katie.

Katie rose through Samantha and into the air. "Rude!"

"Sorry," I thought to her. "She's new."

"I don't like her already." Katie glared at Samantha.

"She doesn't get any better from here."

"Why would she?"

"Hey," Samantha said. "Did you just get the chills?"

I smiled a knowing smile. I had seen enough movies to know that moving through ghosts gave you the chills but didn't know it was true until that moment. "I don't know what you're talking about. You're crazy."

Chapter 16

"I think it was a ghost," Samantha said as she sat down across from me at lunch.

"Yeah, we need to talk about this," I said. "I was being nice the other day, but I like to eat alone."

"No, I get it," Samantha said, taking my lunch bag without asking. "Everybody else here sucks, though. I know you can't argue with that."

I shook my head. "No, I cannot."

"I was wrong," Katie said to me. "I like her."

"You would," I said out loud, forgetting she could hear my thoughts.

"What was that?" Samantha said.

"Nothing," I replied. "You were saying about ghosts."

"Yeah." She opened the bag of chips. "They say that you're supposed to feel it when they pass through you, and it sends a shiver down your spine, and that's exactly what I felt."

"Tell her I didn't walk through her," Katie said in a huff. "She sat on me."

"And get this," Samantha continued. "I overheard a couple of kids saying that they felt a shiver too when they came into the school this morning."

"Hey!" Katie said. "That was me too. Do you think we can use her, Anna? I think we can use her. Maybe we can use her," Katie hovered around next to Samantha and blew into her ear. "Ask her what she knows about ghosts."

"What do you know about ghosts?" I asked Samantha.

Samantha snapped her neck toward Katie. "See. What was that? I felt it again."

My eyes ping-ponged between Samantha and Katie. I hoped that Samantha didn't notice, but her eyes went wide, and I could see that she noticed me looking at Katie.

"What was that?" Samantha pointed her fingers at my eyes.

"Nothing," I replied.

"Just tell her," Katie said. "Maybe she can help."

"Shut up," I growled under my breath.

"That right there." Samantha pointed again. "That wasn't to me, was it?"

"I don't know what you're talking about," I replied, shaking my head vigorously.

"Fine, but I think you know more that you're letting on. I think you know what's going on here, and I'm going to figure out what that is."

"You're crazy," I said, not looking at her.

"Then why do you want to know what I know about ghosts, huh?"

"I was just trying to make conversation!" I shouted, pushing myself up from the table and storming out of the cafeteria. Everybody watched me go, but I didn't care. If I said another word then Samantha was going to know the truth, and I couldn't let her think I was any crazier than she already did.

I ended up sitting on the floor in my secret bathroom on the second floor. The place that only Katie and I knew about, so I wasn't surprised that she found me there after I locked the door.

"I'm sorry," Katie said. "I was just trying to have fun."

"This is not normal," I said, leaning my head back against the wall. "If anybody finds out that I'm talking to you…I don't even know what's going to happen to me, okay?"

"I won't do it again," Katie said, floating down next to me as I curled myself in a ball on the floor. "But I do think Samantha can help."

"Of course you do."

"What's that supposed to mean?" Katie asked, slightly offended.

"You always see the good in people, okay? Even when they abandoned you, you never got mad at them or anything. You just thought everybody was the best."

"That's because everybody *is* the best," Katie replied.

"Your friends didn't come to your funeral, you know? Nobody came, except for like ten people."

"So what? I didn't go to it, either. Why should they be expected to go and be bummed out?"

"How can you be so cool about the fact nobody came to your funeral?"

"I had a lot of time to think about death while I was dying. One of the nice things about being terminal is that it allows you to get your house in order. I made peace with it."

I pushed myself up from the ground. "There you go, looking at the positive in all of this again."

"And you're looking at the negative. That's why we need Samantha. She's like our neutral, like a neuron. She can help balance us out. Besides…"

"Besides what?"

Katie rolled her eyes. "Besides she's kind of cute, okay? Sue me."

I laughed. "Fine, but if I get committed, you're stuck haunting me forever."

"Deal," Katie said. "But if you get committed, we have failed, and the whole world is doomed. So don't get committed, okay?"

"I wasn't planning on it."

The lunch bell rang as I was walking back to the cafeteria and I managed to catch up with Samantha on her way to class.

"All right," I said.

"That's weird. Did you think I would know what you were thinking when you walked up to me, weirdo? I'm going to need more than 'all right.'"

I wrung my hands as I walked. "I'm sorry I ran out so fast."

Samantha nodded. "That's a start."

"I'm weird."

"I know."

"If you want to know what I know, and why I'm being even extra weird right now, then you have to come with me after school."

"Are you going to murder me?"

"No," I said. "But I am going to lead you into the woods. That might make it seem like I'm going to murder you, but I'm not."

Samantha gave me a side-eyed look. "That sounds like the type of thing somebody who was going to murder me would say."

"It sure does, but you'll know I won't murder you when I don't murder you."

She smiled and raised her eyebrows. "I'll be kept in suspense until then."

I shrugged. "If that's what it takes to get you there."

"And what if I don't come? Because this is weird and you're freaking me out."

"If you don't come, then you won't know, but I'm not going to answer any questions. I need your help, and for some reason we think you can help us."

"Who's 'we?'"

I sped up and called over my shoulder. "All questions will be answered after school."

Katie floated past me as I walked to class. "I think you thoroughly freaked her out."

"Yeah," I whispered with a smile.

"You're hoping she doesn't meet us after school, aren't you?"

"I'm hoping she never talks to me again," I thought to Katie.

"Well, I hope you're wrong."

"You would," I thought before stepping into class. In just a couple of hours, we would find out just how much weirdness Samantha was willing to endure.

Chapter 17

I didn't want Samantha to help us, and thought I did a pretty good job scaring her off from ever talking to me again. For all I knew, I might have been saving her life. She wouldn't have to be the victim of the Anna curse.

I certainly didn't expect to see her leaning against the flag pole, tapping her foot, when I came out of the front door.

"Where have you been?" she asked, pushing herself upright. "I've been waiting."

I scratched my head. "I didn't think you would show up."

She raised one eyebrow. "You told me you would show me why you're acting like a freak. I am endlessly fascinated by freaks. Of course I was going to show up."

Katie smiled a gleeful smile as we walked toward the bus. "I knew she was going to show up."

I ignored her and turned back to Samantha. "Let's go then. By the way, I'm not driving you home."

"That's fine," Samantha said. "I actually have a car. I was wondering if you wanted a ride."

"You really want a ride," Katie said to me.

"What kind of car is it?" I asked.

"It's a 1991 piece of garbage," Samantha said with a shrug. "It doesn't even have airbags. But it will get us where we want to go, assuming it doesn't stall out trying, or get hit by anything."

"Sounds safe."

"Well, safer than a school bus. Those things don't even have seat belts."

"All right," I said, walking back over to her. "Let's go."

"Follow me."

Samantha's car wasn't as bad as she made it out to be. It was small, but so were all hatchbacks. It was clean, though, and while it didn't have any bells or whistles, it didn't smoke as she drove it either. I figured that was about all you could ask from a car.

"I hope you don't mind classic rock," Samantha said, turning on Pandora and tossing her phone in the cup holder. "I don't have a radio, but the cup holder amplifies the sound from the speaker."

It didn't, at least not enough for me to hear anything. Still, Katie seemed happy in the back seat bopping along to whatever she could make out from Kenny Loggins' "Danger Zone."

"Did you bring this car from your last home?" I asked as she drove.

"No," she replied. "We were stationed in Germany. I didn't have a car there and it sucked. First thing I did when we moved here was buy this thing with every dollar I saved up for the last sixteen years."

"Was it nice? Germany?"

"It was fine." Samantha didn't take her eyes off the road. "I could drink alcohol, which was cool."

"You can drink here, too. Kids do it all the time."

"Yeah, but I could do it legally there, which was weird. Nothing kills a buzz like drinking with your mom. I prefer pot anyway. It's more mellow."

"I have never smoked."

"Shut up. What else is there to do in this tiny town? I have driven around for days and I couldn't find three cool things."

"Movies, and stuff. I don't know. I haven't really had the most typical high school experience."

"Why not?"

I looked back at Katie and then back to the road. "Make a left up here."

Samantha didn't press me, which I appreciated. Instead, she turned the car to the left and turned onto my street. "Nice houses. Way nicer than the place we're renting."

"Thanks. I had nothing to do with it, though. It was all my parents." I pointed as we approached my house. "It's up here on the right. The light purple one that needs a paint job. Mom won't be home for a while, so you can park in the driveway."

After Samantha parked, I led her to the end of my street, which dead ended in a cul-de-sac, with the woods stretching out for miles behind it. They wanted to build a house on the lot by the woods, but nobody bought it after a bunch of people protested, so they decided to let the woods overtake the property.

"This is far less creepy than you made it out to be," Samantha said. "I was expecting pentagrams and hexes and such. That would have been pretty cool, honestly."

"Well, I didn't want you to come, so there's that."

"Be nice," Katie said to me.

"That's fair. Listen, I know you don't want to talk about it," Samantha said. "But I kinda know all about you, so maybe I can just ask you a couple questions."

"How do you know everything about me?"

"I didn't say everything, but it's a small school and people talk, especially high schoolers. You're kind of famous."

"Is that why nobody talks to me?"

"No," Samantha said, stepping over a log. "I think it's because they fear death and you're marked with it. It's all over you."

"And you don't fear death?"

"Lots of my dad's friends died, and when you're a military kid you get to deal with the fact that Daddy might not be coming home. It's a looming threat, so you just kind of live with it."

"I have lived with the looming threat of death my whole life."

"Even before Katie?"

"Even before Katie. People I love have been dying on me since I was a baby. Most of the time I feel cursed."

"You're not cursed," Samantha said, snapping a twig with her shoe as she walked behind me. "People just die. It sucks."

"Yeah, well lots of people around me died. All I have is Mom and Joanne left."

"Joanne, that's Katie's mother, right?"

"Do we have to talk about this?" I asked with a deep sigh.

"I want to hear about it," Katie said. "Let her talk. Engage with her. Please. For me."

"Yes," I responded to Samantha. "Joanne is Katie's mother. She kind of became my mother too, after my Dad died."

"And Katie…she like, just died, right?"

I nodded. "She just died."

"And I'm sitting in her seat in Hooper's class?" Samantha gulped loudly.

"You are." I nodded again, staring straight forward.

"Wow, I can see why you hate me."

"I don't hate you."

"Please don't lie to me."

I chuckled. "Fine. I kind of hate you, but I kind of like you, too. But I can't let you get too close. I'm trying to protect you."

"From what?"

"From me. From whatever it is within me that makes people die."

Samantha laughed. "You're kind of full of yourself. Did you know that?"

"I am not!" I threw my hands in the air. "Why would you say that?"

"You think death gives a shit about you? It doesn't care about you. It's just something that happens, and sometimes you have the bad luck to be caught in its path."

There was nothing I could say to that. We were completely silent for a long moment before Katie broke in.

"Holy crap," she said. "That was almost profound. I really like her, Banana. Please let me keep her."

I stopped and turned to Samantha. "What I have to show you is just up ahead, but I have to warn you about something."

"Whatever it is, I'm ready."

I took in a deep breath. "I'm not sure that I'm ready to see it again. And I'm not even sure you're going to be able to see it. It's very possible I'm hallucinating."

"You're not!" Katie said.

I raised my eyebrows. "How would you know? That's exactly what a hallucination would say."

"Okay, now you're freaking me out a little," Samantha said. "Who are you talking to?"

"Katie," I said. "She came to me a few nights ago and told me there was a hole that opened in the fabric of space that separated Earth from somewhere called the Dark Place. She told me that the hole is opening fast, and I have to help her stop it." I stopped to look at Samantha, to see the horror in her eyes, but that's not what I saw. She was looking at me with utter fascination. "You're not freaking out?"

She shook her head. "This all seems completely logical to me."

"So, you believe me?" I snapped my fingers. "Just like that?"

"Yup."

"And if you don't see this hole in space, are you going to turn me in to the authorities for being crazy?"

"Authorities don't work that way," Samantha said, stepping on some crunchy leaves. "Now, you said it's just up ahead?"

Katie floated down toward me. "See, I told you she was the right person to help us."

"We'll see about that," I said. "It's in the clearing up ahead."

But I didn't need to tell her. By the time I caught up to her I could tell that she saw the hole to the Dark Place. Her eyes were wide as saucers, watching the blue flames dance in and out of the hole, which had grown to the size of the clearing now.

"You see it, right?" I asked.

"I see everything," Samantha said, nodding. She didn't take her eyes off the Dark Place. "It's beautiful and haunting all at once."

Katie floated in front of Samantha. Her dull blue turned into an electric neon as she closed her eyes and hummed to herself. When she opened her eyes, a burst of light exploded in front of us and both Samantha and I fell backwards to avoid it.

"Hi, Samantha," Katie said, waving at her.

Samantha looked up, blinked a few times, then waved back. "Hi."

Katie's face was grim. "We have a lot of work to do. I hope you can help us."

"I'll try," Samantha said. "If there's anything I can do to help you, I'll try to do it."

"Excellent," Katie said. "Because, honestly, we're lost, and can use all the help we can get."

Chapter 18

"I have a confession to make," Samantha said. We were walking out of the woods. "I'm kind of a witch. That's how I knew so much about ghosts, and why I knew you were talking to one."

"Ah," Katie said, floating next to her. "Well, I'm a ghost, so that doesn't surprise me."

"That wasn't my confession," Samantha said. "My confession is that I always thought it was a bit of hokum, magic and all. We talked about it a lot when I was in Germany, but I've never seen it myself."

"If you thought it was bunk, why did you get into it?"

Samantha shrugged. "I don't know. It made me feel better after my dad's death. The more I learned about death, the less I feared it, and the more I learned about witchcraft, the more powerful I felt, even if deep down I thought it was all bunk. But this…it's like being smacked in the face with proof that magic exists."

"I thought it was bunk, too," I replied, leading from the front, "until I saw Katie and the hole to the Dark Place. Although saying this proves that magic exists is a bit much, don't you think?"

Samantha turned to Katie without breaking her gait. "Are you kidding me? Souls are the best magic, and Katie's ghost proves all the rest of it is true, at least to some extent."

"I don't know about that one," Katie said. "We spent a lot of time researching ghosts and such, and we couldn't find anything that connected it to magic."

Samantha arched her eyebrow. "That's because you didn't know where to look."

"Well, that's obvious. I didn't even know witches were a real thing until like, three minutes ago." I stepped onto the asphalt of the street. "I mean, I guess some people in school are Wiccan, but they don't practice real magic."

"Luckily, you have me now so I can lead you to the truth about magic," Samantha said. "Man, you made a really good decision, bringing me in, whichever one of you decided to do it."

"It was me," Katie said.

Samantha smiled. "I knew that, somehow. Probably since Anna hated me."

"Anna didn't hate you. She's just scared to let anybody into her life. Isn't that right, Banana?"

"Banana?" Samantha chuckled.

"You call me that, and you're dead to me," I grumbled. "Katie can barely get away with it, and I've known her almost my entire life."

"And my entire death, too," Katie added.

"Which is why she gets away with it," I said. "You don't have that luxury."

"Whatever you say."

Samantha drove us across town to her house. Her house was a lot smaller than ours. A small, unassuming porch led into the family room and a small kitchen.

"Mom's room is down the hall," she said, pointing. "I'm this way."

Samantha pushed open the first door on the left. Inside, the room was painted black, with multiple pentagrams drawn on the wall.

"Why do you have so many pentagrams?" I asked.

"To ward off evil spirits." She shrugged. "Stupid superstition which I guess turned out to be right in the end. I thought they looked cool."

"Is it safe for me to come in?" Katie asked.

"Are you evil?"

"Not that I know of," Katie replied.

"Then it should be fine."

Katie slowly hovered into the room with her eyes closed. When she was through the threshold, she opened her eyes and relaxed her shoulders.

Samantha watched her. "Guess you're not evil, then. Sit wherever."

I took a seat on a purple bean bag chair in the corner while Samantha walked toward her bookshelf. She had quite a collection of cheap-looking paperbacks with a few old, leather-bound volumes mixed in as well. She knelt to the bottom shelf, where some of the thickest and oldest looking books rested.

"You have a lot of books," I said.

"It was the only thing I shipped overseas with me. I became obsessed while I was in Germany. Mom wanted me to let it go, but I saved my money from work until I had enough to pay for them to come over myself."

"Have you tried any spells?" Katie asked.

"Not really," Samantha said. "A few wards and such. None of them seemed to do much of anything, though. Of course, I'm not very powerful. I've been working to channel my mana and build my ability well for a while now."

"Excuse me?" Katie said.

"You only have so much energy to do magic. You burn through it, you have to recharge. The more powerful the spell, the more powerful you have to be to cast it, just like a video game."

"Do you think your books will tell us how to close the puncture to the Dark Place?"

"I don't know. Honestly, some of these books I haven't read in a while. But if I can't find it, I know where to go."

"Where?" Katie asked.

"There's a store three not far from my house that sells potions and elixirs to witches. It was one of the first places I found when I got to town. Sold a couple of my favorite books there to raise the rest of what I needed to get my car."

"Can we help?" Katie said.

Samantha pulled a book from the shelf and tossed it to me. "Get reading. Look for anything that can help, no matter how small."

Chapter 19

"This is so boring," I groaned after reading through my seventh witchcraft textbook in an hour. "It's like they don't even know how to write."

"What do you expect?" Samantha said. "It's not like a Nancy Drew mystery."

"Nancy Drew mystery?" Katie gave Samantha a sidelong look.

"What? Don't act all high and mighty. They were super fun to read. Don't hate just because I know good writing."

"I've just never heard somebody admit they read Nancy Drew is all."

I laughed to myself, hearing Katie rib Samantha. There was a time before Katie was sick when I would hang out with her and her friends. Being in Samantha's room felt very much like I was with friends, and nothing was wrong with the fact that a ghost, a witch, and I were trying to close a hole in the universe.

Samantha slammed her book closed. "I think we have to admit that my extensive library doesn't have the information we need."

"I think it's fair to assume that," Katie said. "Even if the information we need was here, I'm too bored to find it."

Samantha pushed herself up from the floor. "I think it's time we took a field trip."

We piled into Samantha's car and drove to a small shop in a strip mall a mile from Samantha's house. It was small and nondescript. I wouldn't have noticed it if Samantha didn't pull up to the front and point to the sign which said

"The Witch's Brew," the words wrapped around a black caldron with a black cat perched on it.

"I think you should stay in the car, Katie," Samantha said as she put the car into park. "I'll be too distracted trying to explain a ghost to the owner."

"Screw that," Katie said. "I'm not waiting in the car for you like a lap dog."

She flew out of the car, and I followed her. "I guess she's spoken, huh? And once Katie makes up her mind on something, you should just go with it."

"Whatever." Samantha took a deep breath and then joined us. A bell jingled when I pressed open the glass door. Inside, the shop was quite dark, and every inch of it was filled with metal shelves with long glass barriers in front of them.

It was far from what I expected. In the movies witch's shops were rustic and cluttered, with weird objects on every wooden surface. There was none of that in the Witch's Brew. It was clean, sterile, and all business. You couldn't touch anything without pushing open the glass doors, and there was no way to open them without a key. It wasn't hard to guess that the person with the key was the tall man in a three-piece suit standing behind the counter.

"May I help you?" The man had a thick, low voice that elongated every word out of his thin lips.

Samantha walked up to the glass counter. "Yes. You're Frank, right?"

"That is my name," the man said. "Unless you want to put a hex on me. Then, it's Humberto."

"Nothing like that. I was in here a couple weeks ago. Sold a couple of books. *Herbs, Lore, and Wisdom of Witches* and *Brewing Potions and You.*"

"Ah yes, already sold them both. Have you brought me others?"

Samantha shook her head. "No. I came because I need your help."

"Ugh. Do you think I just give away my knowledge for free? I'm a very important man, you know. I could charge a lot for what's in my head."

"I'm sure you could," Samantha said. "But I'm not swimming in cash. So how about I ask you my question, and then you can tell me how much you would charge to answer it?"

"Hmmm…an interesting proposition. I accept."

"Have you ever heard of a spell that could repair a rift between life and death?"

"Like, to make you immortal."

"No," I said, shaking my head. "Not like that. Like, imagine the universe popped like a balloon, and there was a big hole that led right to death."

"Ah, you mean the Dark Place, what we in the business call the immortal realm of death. The Dark Place, where we shall slumber forever once our work is done on Earth, and where my beloved waits for me."

"I'm sorry to hear that," Samantha said, dropping her head.

"Death will come for all of us, that is one of the few truths of life."

"True that," I nodded. "So, imagine there was a hole that led from Earth to the Dark Place. Do you know how to repair a hole like that?"

Frank stroked his chin for a moment. "Possible, but you are asking for very old magic. Very dark. Very powerful. I fear you are not strong enough to wield such a spell without burning alive."

"How about you worry about you, Frank," Samantha said. "And let us worry about casting a spell."

"I would, but I'm afraid I cannot, as I only know the name of the spell, and two of its components, but not the whole thing."

"How is that possible?" I asked.

"It's a closely guarded secret. Only a small group of witches knows how to cast that level of magic, and I have not yet been able to infiltrate their ranks."

"He must not be a very powerful witch, then," Katie said with a chuckle.

"I most certainly am," Frank snapped, looking directly at her. "Did you think I did not notice you there, in the corner. I was simply being polite to let you carry about in silence."

My mouth dropped open. "How did you—"

"As I said, I am a very powerful witch. All witches can detect ghosts when they have acquired enough mana to do so. The Council of Witches just hasn't seen me at my full strength. I promise you though, I am powerful enough to cast the spell you seek, and I know a little about it myself, through my own research."

"What's the name of the spell then?" Katie asked, hovering forward.

"So you nitwits can cast it and blow yourselves up? Please. I'm no fool."

"Then what if we work together?" Samantha said. "To cast the spell, I mean."

"Interesting." Frank stroked his chin. "Very well if you can find me what I need, then I will help you decipher the rest of the spell…on one condition."

"What's that?" I asked.

"In return for my help, you must let me drain a vial of ectoplasm from your ghost friend. It's very rare, and I am in desperate need of it."

I looked over at Katie. She shrugged. "We're literally nowhere now, so I guess we have no choice."

I turned back to Frank. "It's a deal."

Chapter 20

Frank pulled a thick three-ring binder off the shelf behind him and flipped through it, stroking his chin with his free hand as he did. With every turn of the page, his indignation grew, until it boiled over.

"Where is it?" he asked, scratching his head. "I know it's in here. Unfortunately, the council keeps high level spells on high guard, but I've been able to decipher a little bit of the spell from old texts and tall tales." He stuck his finger on the next page. "Here we are. The first ingredient is a goblin's toenail."

"Goblin toenails," I said. "Gross."

"No more than any of the other ingredients we witches use for potions, I assure you of that," Frank said. "Now, I know I have a recipe to capture a goblin around here somewhere."

"You're kidding, right?" I asked. "A goblin? Here?"

"And why not?" Frank replied. "Ghosts are real. Why not goblins? I think you will find there are many things that you have taken for fiction truly that exist in this world. Some are innocent while others are so horrible, they would make your hair stand on end."

"That's a stretch," I said. "I mean, I barely believe Katie's real."

"Still?" Katie replied.

"I said barely believe. I believe it with my eyes, but my brain still has its doubts."

"I'm afraid you will have to believe, and soon," Frank said. "Ah, here we go. Goblins hate humans, but they have been known to be lured by a certain combination of flavors baked into a pie." He unclipped the binder and pulled out the sheet of paper, then handed it to me. "Here you are."

"Rhubarb and sweet kidney pie?" I said. "This looks disgusting."

"I agree," Frank said, nodding profusely. "I have tried to bake it a dozen times, but no matter what I do, I cannot tempt the goblin to entreat with me."

"I'm not surprised they avoid you." Katie wrinkled her nose. "Who would eat this?"

"Goblin palates are very different than ours. This is a delicacy to them."

"And we should believe you, even though this recipe didn't work for you?" Katie said.

"Yeah," I added. "Don't you think maybe the reason they haven't come around is because this stuff is putrid?"

"If you have any better ideas, I'd love to hear them," Frank said. "But right now, this is the only recipe I know to capture a goblin, and the spell says that's what we need. You're welcome to walk out any time."

I didn't have a better idea, and he knew that I didn't, and neither did Samantha or Katie. They just looked at me, bewildered. So, we had to try Frank's disgusting pie.

"Fine," I said. "We'll do it."

"Splendid," Frank said, turning around. "Now, when you've baked the pie, make sure to place it inside this cage." Frank pulled a rusted metal bird cage off the shelf behind him and handed it to Samantha. "This cage is enchanted to ensnare a goblin. They can turn invisible at a moment's notice and disappear at will. If you don't catch them in this cage, they will escape. Understand?"

I nodded. "I get it."

"Good," Frank said. "Well, this has turned into quite the interesting day, don't you think?"

"Sure," Katie said with a smile. "I'm excited about catching a goblin. Sounds fun."

Samantha led us out of the store and back into her car. She threw the bird cage into the trunk of the hatchback before getting into the driver's seat.

"Was Frank pretty worthless?" Samantha asked. "Or completely worthless?"

"I liked him," Katie said.

I rolled my eyes. "You like everybody."

"That's because everybody is wonderful. Look, before we went into Frank's store, we had no way to save the world, and now we have the makings of a quest."

"Yes, to catch a goblin, not to close a portal."

"Sounds like a delightful first step. And you know that quests often start with mundane, little tasks before they unfold in front of us into something grander."

Samantha smiled. "You really do love everything, don't you?"

"I really do," Katie said.

Samantha drove us to the nearest Albertson's and led us inside. "You two handle the giblets and meats. I'll handle the sweet things."

"Why do I have to do it?" I made a face. "That stuff is gross."

"Because I drove."

"I guess that's fair," I said, even though I didn't like it.

Samantha strolled off toward the bakery, while I walked down the aisle toward the butcher shop in the back of the supermarket.

Katie followed me. "This is fun, isn't it?"

"I wouldn't go that far," I grumbled.

"Oh, well that's probably because you've been normal your whole life. Think about it from my perspective though. For the last three months of my life, I couldn't move from my bed, and now I'm on an adventure."

I stopped in the middle of the ice cream. "I hadn't thought of that. I'm a horrible friend."

"No," Katie said, turning around. "You're a great friend, just one who misses the forest for the trees. I mean, I never thought I would see you again, Banana, and look at us now, we're inseparable again."

I wanted to reach out and touch her, but that was impossible. If I tried, I would just stumble through her down the aisle. Still, I held my hand out, and watched Katie place hers on top of mine. I felt a slight chill on my fingers from hers.

"I missed you so much."

Katie smiled. "I missed you too. I missed you so much that I…" she trailed off. "Never mind."

"No, tell me."

"I'm ashamed to admit it."

"Please," I said with a smile. "For me."

"I missed you so much, I'm afraid that I tore open the hole to the Dark Place."

"What? That's crazy."

"I don't know," Katie said. "The hole opened right next to me. It could have opened anywhere, but it ripped open right next to me, just when I was thinking about you really hard."

"We're going to fix this," I said. "I promise."

Katie smiled. "Then we better get started."

Chapter 21

"Excuse me," I said, walking up to the butcher. "Do you have any of the gross parts of the chicken here?"

The butcher turned away from his meat slicer toward the counter. He had a hair net holding his long beard like a bib, and thick glasses that made his eyes beady and dark.

"Like what?" he asked with a thick Canadian accent.

"Like organs and junk." I looked down at the recipe. "Specifically, the heart, kidneys, and liver."

"You know, those aren't the disgusting parts. They're actually really tasty, and good for you."

"Sure," I said. "I'm sure they're great, but they look disgusting. This really isn't a semantics lesson. Do you have any or not?"

"You know, most butchers don't," the butcher, said walking behind a partition. "Luckily, we're not most butchers. We get the whole animal fresh from the slaughterhouse and carve it up, so yeah, I have plenty. How many do you need?" I looked at Katie, who gave a bewildered stare.

"Like, a handful maybe?"

"Two pounds," Samantha said over my shoulder. "Can I really not trust you to handle a simple task?"

"I was doing it!" I said to her.

The butcher came out from behind the partition a couple seconds later with a bag full of chicken hearts, livers, and lungs. He slapped a price tag on the bag and handed them to me.

"There you go," he said with a smile.

"How can you do that?" I looked at the disgusting bag of organs in my hand. "How can you smile when you're handing me this bag of guts?"

He shrugged. "I don't know. I just love it is all."

"That's awesome," Samantha said, smiling. "Find a thing you love and do it until you die, right?"

He nodded. "I'm trying."

We paid for our "food" and drove away. Mom was already at work, which meant my house would be empty for hours, so it was the best place to make the pie.

"Are you a cook?" Samantha asked me as we walked into my kitchen.

I pulled out a pan from under the stove. "I am not. Katie wanted to be a chef, but she…"

"I died before I could go to culinary school," Katie said flatly.

Samantha set the bag of innards down on the table. "Do you think it needs to taste good in order for goblins to eat it?"

I took a bowl from the cupboard. "Good to us or good to them?"

"I don't know. I've never done anything like this before." Samantha pulled the recipe out of her back pocket and read it. "The most I've done is cook a pie for my elementary school's bake sale."

"We've never cooked for a magical creature either," Katie said. "I say we just follow the instructions and hope for the best."

"These instructions never did Frank any good," Samantha said.

"Yeah," Katie said. "But we have something he didn't."

"And what's that?" Samantha asked.

"Hope."

"Ugh," I said. "Make me retch."

I had no interest in cooking, but I also had no interest in dying from a giant hole in the universe gobbling us up, so Samantha and I dug in while Katie guided us through the recipe.

Two hours later we had what looked vaguely like a pie, though it stunk to high heaven. "You're lucky you can't smell this, Katie."

"For once," Katie said, "my death has been a benefit for something."

We placed the pie into Frank's enchanted cage and headed out into the woods at the end of my block. The instructions under the recipe were very specific to bring the cage to an opening in the woods and wait for the goblin to appear.

"Is here good?" Samantha asked. She set the cage down in the center of the clearing several hundred yards away from the Dark Place. It had doubled in size since the last time I saw it. Soon, it would devour the whole woods and everything around it.

"I don't know," Katie said. "Seems as good as anywhere."

"Open the cage and get over here," I called to Samantha.

She opened the latch on the cage and walked back to where I was standing at the edge of the clearing. There was nothing to do but wait and hope that goblins liked our disgusting pie.

Chapter 22

After two hours of waiting without capturing a goblin, we figured we had either been suckered or duped. Either way, we knew there were no goblins coming to eat our pie, and so we walked back to my house, defeated.

"Well, that was a waste of time," Samantha said as she slammed the cage on the kitchen counter. "I'm going to punch that guy right in the face tomorrow."

"It's not his fault," I replied. "He's just an idiot. We're the ones that believed him. The real blame is on us."

"We'll figure it out," Katie said. "We only tried it one time. If we try again tomorrow, maybe in a different spot, we could still catch that goblin, no problem."

"And how many more times will we have to try this before the Dark Place gobbles us up?" Samantha said. "That hole is getting bigger every day.

"Don't think about that now," Katie said. "We'll try again tomorrow."

"Whatever," Samantha said. "I'm going home."

It was for the best that Samantha left. I wanted to be alone with Katie. I didn't know how much more time we had together, and I wanted to cherish every precious second.

"I dare you to eat it," Katie said as we stared down at the pie.

"That's disgusting," I said. "It smells like old feet."

"So what? You made it. You should eat it."

I gave her a sidelong glance. "What will you give me for it?"

"I don't know what I possibly have that you want."

"One page of your diary. I want to read one page of your diary."

"That's a tall order, hombre."

I pointed down at the pie. "And this is totally disgusting, so I think it's a fair trade. You want me to eat it, you gotta give up the goods."

Katie bit her lip. "Fine. One page, but I get to choose the page."

"Then we have a deal."

I walked over to the utensil drawer and pulled out a fork. It was going to be disgusting, but it would be worth it. I would have done just about anything to get a peek at that diary.

I stepped back over to the cage and dipped my fork in the disgusting pie. The filling smelled curdled. I pressed the fork to my lips and forced the meat inside my mouth. I nearly wretched as I chewed it up.

"No vomiting, or the deal is off," Katie said, laughing.

"You can't change the deal mid-bite." I choked on the words as bits of meat and pie crust flung out of my mouth.

"Well, I just did." She folded her arms across her chest with a smug smile.

I ran over to the sink and stuck my mouth under the faucet. I turned on the spigot and drank every ounce of water that came out of it, until I had swallowed the last remnants of the pie.

"That was horrible," I said, gagging and trying not to retch.

"But you did it, and you can feel okay about that. You accomplished something, even though that something was disgusting."

"I feel horrible about it, but at least it means I get to read your diary now."

Katie peered at me with squinted eyes. "Why are you so interested in my diary? You can ask me anything you want. I'm floating right here."

"I know, but people tend to lie in person. They don't lie to their diaries."

"Are you sure about that? I feel like I lied to my diary more than I ever lied to you."

"Why?"

Katie dipped her head. "Because that diary was going to be around a lot longer than me, and I wanted to look good when somebody found it."

"That doesn't make any sense. Why would you hide it if you wanted somebody to find it?"

"I didn't say I wanted somebody to find it, but I knew they would, eventually," Katie said, turning toward the sink. "This isn't an interrogation."

"No, it's not. I'm sorry." I took a cautious step toward her. "Look, if you don't want me to read your diary, I won't."

She shook her head. "No, a deal is a deal."

I knocked softly on Joanne's door, confident that the light from the TV through the front window meant she was still up. It was late, but I figured she'd be awake. She didn't sleep much when Katie was alive and had maintained the habit of staying up until all hours of the night.

"Hi," I said when she opened the door. I was taken aback by the tears in her eyes. Joanne rubbed at them with a wad of tissues.

"I'm sorry, Anna. This really isn't a good time."

"It's never a good time," I said. I looked over at Katie, whose heart would have broken at the sight of her shattered mother if she still had a heart to break. "It's lonely over there, Joanne, and I would rather not be alone right now, if that's okay."

Joanne smiled through her tears. "As long as you're okay with being around a blubbering mess."

"It's never bothered me before."

I stepped over the threshold and into the living room. I was on a mission to find and read Katie's diary, but missions change all the time, and I couldn't just leave Joanne to her pain.

"What are we watching?"

"Hallmark movies," Joanne said. "I know they're corny, but there's something nice about knowing that nothing bad will ever happen to anybody in them."

"Mom watches them, too, when I'm not around. She thinks I'm going to make fun of her, but secretly I love them, too. So did Katie. I would stay up all night watching them with her, when we weren't watching horror movies, of course. It was a weird combo, but Katie was weird like that."

Joanne nodded slowly. "I remember her asking me if we could move to Kern County after watching Jennifer Love Hewitt in one of those movies."

"It was Bucks County, and it was Lacey Chabert," I corrected her.

"I'm pretty sure it was Jennifer Love Hewitt."

"No, Mom," Katie said. "It was Lacey Chabert."

For a moment, Katie forgot that she was a ghost, and that her mother couldn't hear her, and she fell into her old rhythm. She caught herself though, and I could see her heart collapse upon itself. She covered her mouth, and hurried off, floating up the stairs.

"It was Lacey Chabert," I said, pushing myself up from the couch. "I'm sure of it."

Chapter 23

I heard Katie crying before I pushed open the door to her room. I didn't know that ghosts could cry, and yet, there she was, with her head in her hands, her back heaving with ugly, blue tears streaming down her face.

"We can cry," Katie said. "We have human emotions, at least until they're leached out of us."

I sat down on the bed next to her. "I didn't know."

"It's okay," Katie said. "I didn't know how hard it would be to stay hidden around her."

"Is that why you didn't show yourself to her?"

Katie nodded. "She can barely handle it now that I'm dead. If she knew I was back, it would give her hope, which would be cruel. She has to heal."

"It's okay," I said, more for me than for her. I couldn't do anything to comfort her. I couldn't rub her back or give her a hug. All I could do was sit next to her and let her cry.

"Besides, I don't think Mom would understand, and if she understood, I think the shock of seeing me again might kill her."

"And you didn't worry about that with me?"

Katie looked over at me. "You're tougher than she is. Mom has been through so much that it's broken her. If she knew I was still here, I don't know if she could ever get over her grief."

"That's a horrible choice you had to make."

"Life is hard. The afterlife is harder, though." Katie sighed deeply. "I think you should get my diary and claim your prize."

"We don't have to do this now."

Katie shook her head. "It's okay. We might as well get it out of the way."

I stood up and lifted the mattress. I pulled out the notebook stuffed underneath and sat back down next to Katie.

"What page do you want me to read?"

"It doesn't matter. Honestly, just read the whole thing if you want."

I shook my head. "A deal's a deal."

"Then just open to any page and start reading, I guess. The further along the sadder it gets though, just warning you."

I cracked the book open. "I'll read a page at the beginning then. We've already had enough sadness for one day."

I flipped through a few pages and then finally stopped on a page with the headline "First Chemo." Around the margins of the paper Katie had drawn little hearts and balloons in pink markers and then started the entry with "Dear Diary."

"That's a good one," Katie said. "You'll enjoy it. It's sad, but not too sad."

Dear Diary,

Tomorrow I have my first chemo appointment. I won't lie and say that I'm sad about it, because in some ways I'm looking forward to it. The cancer isn't going away on its own. The only way to stop it is to fight back.

Anna offered to come with me, even though it will be painfully boring. She is a true friend.

None of my other friends offered to come with me. I'm trying not to feel too bad about it, but it hurts to know none of them will sit by my side.

I looked up at Katie, who was watching me. "I knew it mattered to you that they didn't come."

"I never said it didn't hurt, just that I didn't hold it against them."

I nodded. "Fair enough."

"Why did you come with me?" Katie asked me as I finished the entry. "I didn't always make time for you back then."

"It didn't matter. You were my friend. We weren't always close friends, at least not then, but you needed me. You hid it well, but I could always see the fear behind your eyes."

She placed her hand above mine, and I felt the chill from her soul on the top of my hand. "I don't know what I would have done without you."

I held up the book toward her. "I should put this back."

"No," Katie said. "Keep it. I thought it would be hard to have you read it, but it was actually nice to show you what I was thinking back then."

I tucked the book under my arm. "I'll treasure it."

My eyes moved up to meet the haunting glow from Katie's eyes. I could see through them and past her, to the window behind her body, but I still felt a connection with her body, and a resonance with her soul, that I had never felt before, even when she was alive.

"Are you okay up there?" Joanne yelled at me from downstairs.

"Be right down!" I called back down to her.

As I stood up, the phone in my pocket buzzed. It was a text from Samantha. *"Get to your computer NOW."*

Chapter 24

I said a quick goodbye to Joanne and rushed across the street. I didn't want to leave her alone in her sad state, but I also wanted to save the world, and in doing so, save Joanne, my mother, and everybody else.

I slid into my chair and logged into my account before finding my chat thread with Samantha on Facebook.

What is it? I asked.

I found an answer. She sent me a link for www.witchynet.com.

What am I looking 4?

Look @ the summoner forum.

I clicked on the link and it took me to a website devoted to witchcraft. Katie and I had found it when we were searching around for answers, but it didn't seem as reputable as any others, so we didn't bother searching around.

OK. I'm there. Now what?

Search for goblins.

I typed goblins into the search field and the first thread was a recipe for summoning goblins. The top of the thread read:

Everything you know about summoning goblins is wrong. If you want to know the right way to summon a goblin, PayPal me $20 and I will tell you what I know.

I texted Samantha. *This is a scam.*

How do u know? she messaged back.

It has 2B

Y?

BC it's on the internet.

> *Well, I hope not, bc I paid her and we're meeting her in 30. Meet me @ Primrose Diner in 15.*

No car

Fine. I'll pick you up.

This sounds stupid, but OK

U have any better ideas? C U in 10.

She was right. I didn't, but that didn't mean I had to like her idea. Still, if it got me a better recipe for finding goblins and allowed me to close the portal to the Dark Place, then I was all for it.

Katie and I waited outside for Samantha to show up. It was a nice night, even if it was a little cold. Katie didn't seem to mind either way, except that every minute the tear to the Dark Place grew bigger.

"Can I ask you something?" I said.

"Sure," Katie replied.

"You said that you caused the rift, but that was just hyperbole, right?"

"I don't know," she said. "All I know is that one moment, I was wishing and praying to see you again, and the next thing I knew a hole opened up next to me and led me back into the woods. That's quite the coincidence."

I thought for a moment. "Ever think that maybe if you wished to go away that it would go away too?"

"I tried that." Katie looked over to the faint blue tint coming from the woods. "But it didn't work."

"Doesn't that kind of tell you it wasn't you in the first place?"

"Maybe." She shook her head. "It doesn't matter. I have to fix it."

"Why do you think nobody's seen it yet? I figured every ghost hunter in the state would have come flocking by now."

"They don't want to see it, just like they don't want to see me. Think about what would happen if everybody in the world saw the rift to the Dark Place or knew there were ghosts. It would be bedlam."

"I don't know. I think most people still wouldn't believe, even if you were staring them in the face."

"Maybe."

"I barely believe, and it's happening to me." Samantha's car turned down the street before Katie could say anything else. "Come on. Let's go."

The Primrose Diner was the oldest restaurant in town. Rosie, the owner, took great pride in that distinction, and in her historical landmark status. To everybody else, though, it was a bit of an eyesore with its bright pink exterior screaming out to everybody driving past. To Rosie, it meant history, or at least that's what she said when people asked why she didn't tear it down—or at least give it some fresh paint or repairs.

I thought it just meant she was cheap, honestly. After all, when something was "historic", it generally meant that people didn't have to clean it up and make it nice. I was sure that nothing had been replaced since she bought the place from her uncle in the '70s, and it was unlikely he'd replaced anything since he opened the place in the '40s.

Still, there was something nice about walking into a place and knowing it was just the same as it was the last thirty times you had been there, and the last thousand times before that. The food was passable, sure, and it was open later than anywhere else in town, so Rosie had a monopoly on late night customers.

"How do you even know about this place?" I asked Samantha as we walked inside.

"Please, I'm new, but I'm not dead." She stole a look at Katie. "No offense."

"None taken," Katie said.

"This is the only place to go when I can't sleep. I've been here almost every night since we moved in."

The checkered-tile floors were sticky with maple syrup. I walked over and slid into a booth that had been patched with duct tape so much the pink vinyl underneath was barely visible. Samantha sat across from me, and Katie hovered at the end of the table.

"She should be here any minute," Samantha said, glancing at the clock on her phone.

"This is crazy, you know," I said. "What makes you think paying somebody you found online is going to be able to help us?"

"Nothing," Samantha said. "But since Frank's plan didn't work, we needed another, and this seemed like a good enough place to start."

"I'm just saying that I wouldn't have paid for some random person's advice."

"Well luckily, you didn't have to pay," Samantha replied.

"I think she's here," Katie said, looking over at the door.

An old woman with thin, gray hair walked into the diner. She wore dozens of layers, with a short burgundy shawl around her shoulders. Her nose was hooked, and when she turned to me, I could see she had lost several of her teeth. The long years of her life were etched on her face with a multitude of wrinkles.

"This must be her," I said, waving my hand in the air.

Samantha looked back. "I'm not sure. She's a bit of a cliché, isn't she?"

"There are clichés for a reason, Samantha."

The old woman noticed my wave and smiled at me. However, soon her smile turned into confusion and puzzlement. She turned to look behind her, then back to me, before scratching her head. A few seconds later, a portly, bald man walked in and took the old woman by the arm.

"Come on, Mom," he said, before dragging her in the other direction. The old woman turned and waved at me with a toothless smile before disappearing into a booth at the other end of the diner.

"Maybe not," Katie said.

"No, I should say not." The shrill voice was coming from the booth behind us. "Honestly, that kind of stereotyping is what got a lot of innocent women burned at the stake."

Chapter 25

A large woman, large in a tall way not in a wide way, stood up from the booth behind us and whipped around to our table. She wore a blue cap with a rose brooch pinned into the felt, and a long, flowing, blue cape which stopped an inch from the ground. It bounced as she moved, as if it had a mind of its own. A purple kerchief was tied around her neck, while her face was made up perfectly, with glowing, red cheeks that matched her fiery lipstick. Her cold, blue eyes bored into my soul as she swept into our booth and sat next to Samantha.

"I would very much thank you not to think of any of those stereotypes when I am around, thank you."

"Are you 'Broom Hilda?'" Samantha asked.

"That is my handle," the woman said. "However, it's more a joke than anything. While my name is Hilda, I do not use a broom. I just happen to enjoy the comic strip very much, as well as a good play on words."

"She looks more like the fairy godmother from Cinderella," Katie said to me under her breath. "Or Mary Poppins."

"I'll take that as a compliment," Hilda said, looking directly at Katie. "However, in the future I would appreciate if you kept the snark to yourself."

Katie gulped loudly. "I'm sorry."

"No need to apologize. If I could remain hidden from humans, who knows what I would say."

"I don't know," I said to her. "I don't know anything about what you've said since you came over here."

"Of course you don't, dear. That's because you are doing this all wrong. Samantha told me all the details over email, except for one. Now, tell me, how did you come across the recipe you use now?"

"We went to a curiosity shop and got it from a witch there."

"A female witch or a male warlock? Please be precise."

"A warlock named Frank," Samantha said.

Hilda looked at the ceiling with an exasperated look. "Of course it would be Frank," she said. "He's been trying to lure a goblin for ages. Of course, he doesn't have the right recipe. Goblins would never go for sweet and savory pie. It's rubbish."

"How do you know Frank?" Katie asked.

"He's the only registered witch within a ten-mile radius, so I had my assumptions. He's been petitioning to get into the high council for years. Never much cared for him though, so we've been sending him on wild goose chases."

Katie frowned. "That's not very nice."

"No, it's not," Hilda said with a small shrug. "However, I could not deal with that man working with me for the rest of eternity. He's so droll. Now, please tell me you aren't trying to harness a goblin for his toenail clippings."

"What does it matter?" I asked. "We paid. Now give it."

"You didn't pay for anything dear, now did you? It was all your friend, the one who shows great potential."

"I do?" Samantha asked, looking surprised.

"Of course, dear, you have a real gift with witchcraft. I can feel it dripping off you. If only you could keep your focus for more than a moment you might get somewhere." Hilda turned to Katie. "Let's take a look at you. I suppose you promised your ectoplasm in return for his help, did you not?"

"I did," Katie said.

"It's a very painful procedure, you know, harnessing your ectoplasm. You must be wrung dry for an hour over a boiling cauldron. Most unpleasant. I doubt you would have agreed to it if you knew the risks."

"Yes, I would have, because I'm trying to save the world."

"And now we come to it," Hilda said. "I suppose you are talking about closing your little rift between Earth and the Dark Place, right?"

"We are," I said, nodding.

"The afterlife is a terrible place, which is why I plan to live forever," Hilda said with a small laugh. "Of course, this tear is nothing to worry about very much. They usually heal themselves in a week or so."

"This one isn't healing itself," Katie said. "It's getting bigger."

"Is it now?" Hilda cocked one eyebrow. "That is concerning."

"Can you close it?"

"Of course I can, my dear, but will I? That is another question. There are many other things that require my attention."

"And this doesn't require your attention?" Samantha asked.

"My dear, you have no idea what powers seek to destroy us even now. This is my fifth highest priority, maybe sixth. Call me when the rift is the size of the national mall."

"If you're not going to do it, then tell us. How do you seal it?" Katie asked.

"Well I suppose I could," Hilda replied. "You just need the right paste, ground from goblin bones, troll mucus, and dragon fire, and bound together with ectoplasm from a ghost."

"We don't have any of those things," Samantha said. "Except the ectoplasm."

Hilda pulled a piece of paper out of her coat. "Well, this should get you started. Instructions on how to really catch a goblin. Watch out though, they are very tricky."

"What do you expect us to do with it once we've caught it?"

"Kill it, of course." Hilda looked around at our horrified faces. "You won't be able to kill it, will you?"

"Why not?" Katie said.

"Well first, just look at you." Hilda chuckled. "A ruddy lot, and not stone-cold killers, are you?"

We looked at each other, but we knew the answer to that question. "No."

"I didn't think so," Hilda said. "No bother. I have a solution for you. If you bring me a live goblin, I will in return give you the ground up bones you require. Deal?"

Samantha nodded. "Deal."

"We're still delivering a living being to its doom, though, aren't we?" Katie asked.

"You ate chicken, beef, and pork while you were alive, didn't you?"

"I guess so," Katie replied.

"This is no different," Hilda said.

"That's depressing," Katie said.

"But true."

"We'll do it," I told Hilda.

"Splendid. Then I will talk to you soon." And with a snap of her fingers, she vanished from the table, leaving us all shaking our heads in wonder. We looked around the diner, but it didn't look like anybody noticed what had happened.

"Can I get y'all something to eat?" A short waitress sidled up to our table. Katie moved away as the waitress walked through her. "Ooh, what a shiver. Now, maybe I can get you some chicken fingers, or eggs and bacon?"

"No," I said, scooting out of the booth. "I think I've lost my appetite."

Chapter 26

The instructions Hilda gave us said that we needed thistle, barley, chicken broth, eggs, and newt eyes. The first four things were easy to find, but the last meant we needed to stop back by the only witch store we knew and talk to Frank.

After school the next day, we paid his shop a visit. Samantha walked in first, and Frank's eyes lit up for a moment. They fell flat when he saw we didn't have the cage.

"Oh," Frank said. "I thought maybe you would be useful or something."

"We were useful," Katie said, floating up to the register. "We got you the REAL recipe for how to catch a goblin."

"Impossible, I paid for that recipe myself. It's from someone on the high council."

"Was it Hilda?" I asked.

He nodded. "Of course. She's been a friend of mine for years. The only one who looked out for me."

"Sorry to tell you, pal," Samantha said, "but she hates you."

"No," Frank said. "That's impossible. She was close with my late wife. We ate dinner together often. My wife even thought of her as a mentor."

"I'm telling you, dude. She hates you."

"It's true," I added.

Katie floated between me and Samantha and said, "We all heard it with our own ears."

"But, I've been working so hard. So hard." Frank slammed his fist on the glass counter. "And she just led me along like I was a stupid puppy?"

I nodded. "It's okay. She gave us a new recipe to try out. All we need are some newt eyes."

"And you think I have them?" Frank scoffed. "Why? Because stupid old movies say that witches use them?"

"Basically," Katie said.

Frank sighed. "I hate that I have to prove you right. Listen, everything you know about witches is wrong, and I don't have time to tell you the truth but mark my words. There is a great conspiracy against witches in the mainstream media. They are trying to subjugate us because—"

"Does that mean you do or don't have newt eyes?" I asked.

Frank knelt under his counter and shuffled around for a moment, before popping up with a canister labeled "pickled newt eyes."

"Don't judge me." Frank set the canister on the corner. "Our agreement still stands. If you get the goblin, you will bring it to me first, so that I can clip its toenails."

"You don't need its toenails," I said. "Hilda told us the real recipe. You need its bones, ground down into a powder."

"That's impossible," Frank replied. "I deciphered that ingredient straight from a broken tablet written in ancient *Luvastitan*…oh…yes…I see the problem. Toenail and bones are very similar in the writing. Well, that would have been embarrassing."

"I'm not sure if I can kill a goblin," Samantha said.

Frank sighed. "It isn't ideal, but the future of the world is at stake."

I nodded. "It's true. I don't see any other choice."

"Bring it to me," Frank said. "I will deal with it myself."

"Are you sure?"

Frank pursed his lips. "No, but I suppose there is no other choice. Like you said, we are trying to save the world."

"Thank you."

"Very well," Frank said, holding out the canister of newt eyes. "I suppose you will need this, then."

"This is so gross," I said, taking it and eyeballing it.

"We also need ectoplasm," Samantha said. "Which Katie is willing to give, except…"

"Except that it's not supposed to be pleasant," Katie said. "Hilda said that you have to drain me for an hour to get ectoplasm and that it hurts."

Frank shook his head. "That's the barbaric way the council does it. I've found a much more humane way to drain a ghost which is no more painful than getting your blood drawn."

"Are you sure?" Katie said hopefully.

"Positive," Frank said. "If you want, I can show you."

"If you hurt her, I'll kill you," I said, gritting my teeth.

"I will be as delicate as possible."

"It's okay," Katie said, moving closer to Frank. "I'll stay here and give Frank the ectoplasm he needs for himself and for the spell. You both go to the woods and find the goblin."

I didn't like this. "Don't get hurt."

Katie nodded. "Not a whole lot somebody could do to me now, Banana."

"Still," I said. "Be careful."

Samantha drove me back to my house and helped me cook the ingredients into a stew. It took most of the evening brewing it according to Hilda's recipe. The instructions said that the broth needed to be served warm, so I poured it into a thermos before Samantha and I made our way back into the woods.

"Do you think this is going to work?" Samantha asked.

I looked over into the woods as the tear into the Dark Place loomed over us. "I sure hope so. I don't know what will happen if we can't close that hole soon."

"I hope so, too. This planet sucks but I kind of like it here."

"Me too," I said with a smile.

When we had walked far enough into the woods that I couldn't see the lights from my house, Samantha set down the enchanted bird cage, and I opened the thermos.

"At least this smells better than the pie," I said. "Tastes better too."

"Yuck, you tasted the pie?"

I walked away from the cage and knelt in the bushes near it. "Katie made me."

"How can a ghost make you do anything?"

"It's not because she's a ghost. It's because she's my friend, and I love her."

Samantha knelt next to me. "You really do love her, don't you?"

"Of course I do. I would do anything for her."

Samantha stared at the cage. "Did you date, when she was alive?"

"No." My eyes dropped to the ground. "I didn't even know she liked me like that until after she was dead."

"And you liked her, I assume."

I bit my lip. "I loved her. I still love her."

"That must be a bummer."

"That's an understatement."

Samantha closed her eyes tightly. "I left my boyfriend in Germany. Hardest thing I ever had to do. Couldn't even imagine what I would do if I couldn't see him again."

"Luckily, I can see her again."

"For now."

I turned to her. "What does that mean? For now?"

Samantha looked up at the hole to the Dark Place. "When we close that up, she'll have to go back, won't she? I mean, we can't just have ghosts hanging around here."

I had never thought about that before. I just assumed she would be back forever, but that wasn't true, was it? If we succeeded, she would have to go back to the Dark Place, forever, and sooner or later she would forget about me, and devolve into a primordial ooze.

Samantha must have recognized my inward struggle, because her face dropped. "I'm sorry, but I thought you knew. I mean—"

She hadn't finished her sentence before the cage snapped closed and started to rattle. I hopped up with Samantha on my heels and chased after the cage as it crashed through the forest.

"Stop!" I shouted to the cage, but it just moved faster. Whatever was inside was making horrible screaming noises like it was having its skin ripped off by a rabid dog.

Samantha sprinted ahead of me and leapt on top the cage. It jumped and banged under her. "Shut up! Shut up! Just calm down!"

The cage gave one last jump and then was still. Samantha picked it up and we looked inside. It was a hairy, little, nasty bugger, with a long-horned nose and warts all over its body. As we watched it guzzle the remnants of the soup we made it, the goblin smiled and vanished from view.

"Where did it go?" I shouted. "I thought this thing was enchanted!"

"It must be invisible. Believe me, it's still in there," Samantha said. "The cage weighs a ton."

"How do we make it uninvisible?"

"Let's just get him back to Frank and figure out the rest of the recipe."

Chapter 27

"Hurry up," I said as we trekked back through the woods. "We have to get this back to Frank ASAP."

We heard a great crash of thunder, and there was a burst of purple smoke in front of us. Out from the smoke stepped Hilda, every bit as perfectly quaffed as she was the last time we saw her, except now her deep blue eyes had turned to red, as had her clothing.

"I don't think that will be necessary," Hilda said. "After all, we had a deal, didn't we?"

I nodded. "We did, but Frank said he could drain Katie's ectoplasm without hurting her."

"Tsk tsk, and you believed him?" Hilda asked, taking a step toward us. "Frank means well, but he's an imbecile. You should not throw your lot in with him. Now, hand over the cage and we will have an end to our arrangement."

Samantha shook her head. "We don't have to give anything to you. I paid you, and in return you gave me a recipe for catching a goblin. Our transaction is complete."

Hilda brushed past me on her way over to Samantha, who was trying her best to hold on to the cage, even though it banged and rattled with the goblin's attempts to escape.

"I'm afraid it's not," the witch said. "There have been some complications, and you will need to come with me."

Samantha shook her head. "I'm not going anywhere with you."

"Oh, poor dear," Hilda said with a dangerous smile. "I'm afraid that wasn't a request." She touched the cage, and there was another flash of lightning. When the smoke cleared, she was gone, along with Samantha and the cage.

"Samantha!" I shouted, but it was no use. She was gone. "Sam!"

I ran over to the spot they had been standing right before they disappeared. There was nothing left except for Samantha's purse and a small vial of white powder with a hand-written note attached to it which read, "Sorry for the trouble. Still, a deal is a deal. Here's the goblin powder."

I grabbed the purse and vial of ground-up goblin bones and ran back to my house. I had no way of communicating with Hilda, except on the forum which Samantha led me to before we first encountered her. I scrolled through the site until I found Samantha's post and clicked on it. A screen popped up that told me I could only access the site if I were a member.

I clicked on the register button at the top of the page, but it took me to a new page that said, *"No new registrations accepted. Please return next January when new applications will be considered."*

"Dang it," I whispered to myself. The only person who could log in was Samantha, and she had been taken by Hilda. I needed to get to her house and find her computer, but I didn't have a way to get over there. Then I remembered that Samantha had a car.

I opened her purse and pawed around until I felt keys and pulled them out. I had my driver's license, but I barely drove anywhere. Still, that didn't mean I couldn't. I ran downstairs and out into the street. I hopped into Samantha's car and turned the ignition.

"Come on," I said under my breath as the car chugged to life.

I put the car into drive and lurched forward onto the street. It had been a while since I'd been behind the driver's seat of a car, so my moves were choppy and unsure, but I made incremental progress toward Samantha's house.

When I got there, I took the keys and tried each one in the door until I found the one that turned the lock. The lights were off, and it didn't look like anyone was home, which was a relief because I wouldn't know how to explain myself. Any explanation I gave would make me sound like a crazy person, anyway.

I ran into Samantha's room and started the computer. Luckily, she didn't have a lock on her computer, and I was able to sign right into her account and open her browser. I typed in the website and logged into her account. Her password was saved by Google Chrome, one of the creepiest and most useful innovations of the technological age.

Again, I scrolled through until I found Hilda's account and clicked on it. This time I was able to send her a message.

Give Samantha back now!

I didn't expect an immediate response, so when I got one it threw me for a bit of a loop.

No. She is my property until I get what I need from her.

Give her back, or I'll find you and make you regret it.

After a few seconds, another response: *I like you. You have the gumption of a witch with none of the training, but you're punching out of your league.*

Chapter 28

I had nowhere left to go except back to the magic shop. There wasn't time to fight with a witch, not when the Dark Place rift was opening more with each minute, but I couldn't let her just keep Samantha, either.

"Frank!" I shouted as I walked into the empty shop. All the lights were turned off. Behind the counter I saw something flickering underneath a locked door. The faint blue light reminded me of Katie's, and my heart jumped into my chest.

I heard a scream from the back—Katie's scream—and I leapt into action. I jumped over the counter and slammed open the door. I expected to see Katie writhing in pain, but instead she was laughing and giggling with Frank.

"And what's that one?" she said, pointing to a three-eyed head suspended in a jar of translucent goo.

"That's a banshee head," Frank replied. "Witches use them to see into the past, but it's very dangerous work. Drives most of them mad, and since we can't change the past, it's generally not worth the hassle. Still, they're good sellers, so I keep them in stock."

"Katie!" I shouted.

Katie turned with a smile. "Banana! You're back!"

That would have been the moment that I wrapped my arms around her, except that there was nothing to wrap my arms around, only her translucent body.

"Where's the other one?" Frank grunted. "And my goblin? What have you done with my goblin?"

"Hilda has her. She took Samantha and the goblin."

"The witch?" Katie asked. "How did she even know where you were?"

"A locator spell, I'm sure," Frank replied. "Hilda puts them on everything. She and her council need to know everything all the time. God forbid there be any mystery in the world."

"You seem a little bit angry about that, Frank," I said.

"I hate the council. They're pompous jerks."

"If you hate it so much, why do you want to be on it so bad?"

"Well, I didn't know they were pompous jerks until you told me Hilda hated me," Frank said. He sounded bitter. "Now, I hate them. They've been off the righteous path for decades now, and I turned a blind eye, but no more."

"Righteous path and witch sound like incongruent concepts," Katie replied.

"It's called the dark arts. Not the evil arts."

"Do you have any idea where Hilda would take her?" I asked.

Frank shook his head. "No, but we have bigger problems, I'm afraid. The rift to the Dark Place is opening wider by the day. We have to stop it as soon as possible."

I pulled the goblin powder out of my pocket and held it up. "This is the goblin bone, and you have the ectoplasm. Now, we need dragon fire and troll mucus."

"There is a troll that lives under Coronado Bridge. Get him to help you. Meanwhile, I will try to track down the dragon fire."

"What about Samantha?" I asked.

"Did Hilda say why she wants her?"

I frowned, unsure. "She said Samantha has something she needs."

Frank stroked his chin. "And does she?"

"I don't know."

"Then we have to work to find her, too, but we must close the rift first. That is our top priority."

"You're not so bad," I said. "I thought you were kind of a jerk, but it turns out you're kind of nice."

"People can be two things at once. Duality is one of the bedrock principles of witchcraft. Two sides of the same coin, and the like. Now go. We don't have much time. The troll will turn back into a rock at daybreak."

Chapter 29

"You can go the speed limit you know," Katie said from the passenger's seat of Samantha's car.

We were driving down the freeway, and every car on the road was zipping past us. I didn't care, however, because I was scared out of my mind to be driving on the highway for the first time since I got my license. Not just a little way down the road either—I was driving all the way from Orange County down to San Diego, which was over an hour of straight highway, so I was taking it slow.

"That's easy for you to say. You're already dead."

"You're not going to kill us."

"No. I'm going to kill me. You're already dead."

"There are so many safety features in cars these days, you probably wouldn't even die if you get hit."

"Can you please stop saying the words die, or dead, or dying, or anything that implies not being alive."

"Sorry," Katie said. "It's just that, well, going too slow is just as dangerous as going too fast."

"That can't be true."

"It is. My mom told me all about it."

"Your mom, the speed demon?"

"It's just as dangerous as going too slow."

Cars swooshed by me on either side and I clenched onto the steering wheel until the blood drained from my white knuckles. "That sounds like the kind of thing people like to say to justify endangering themselves."

Katie didn't stop complaining until we pulled off the highway, but we reached San Diego before daybreak, and made our way to the Coronado Bridge. The bridge led from the mainland of San Diego to Coronado Island. There wasn't much to do on the island except visit an old arcade or look out at the ocean, but people liked to do it all the same. I never imagined there was magic under the bridge.

There wasn't an easy way down from the top of the bridge to the sand below it, but we found an access road that led to a switchback which let us slowly work our way down to the bottom of the bridge. We couldn't bring Samantha's car down all the way to the bottom of the bridge, so we had to make the rest of the way on foot. By the time we stepped foot on the sand, the yellow-orange of sunrise was mixing with the blue of the night. We were almost out of time.

"Hurry up," Katie said as I rushed along the sand. There was a homeless camp set up at the bottom of the bridge. Homeless people were a problem in southern California, but they never bothered me. I thought they were smart. If I had to be homeless anywhere, I would want to be in a place with easy access to the ocean and very little rainfall.

"We're never going to find him in this crowd," Katie said, throwing her arms in the air. There must have been two hundred homeless people at the base of the bridge, mulling around, eating scraps of food from flaming trash can grills, and trying to get some shut eye before the sun rose again.

"Excuse me," I asked a tall, greasy man with straggly hair. "Have you seen a troll around here?"

"Lots of trolls around here, love," a greasy man with bright blue eyes said. "Look around. Men ugly and mean enough to grind your bones and eat ya for dinner."

"Sure," I said. "I don't doubt that, but I mean a real troll. Like the kind who lives under bridges and takes coin for passage in exchange for not eating you."

"Nah, I don't know nobody like that, not that they would get a lot of coin around here."

"Look over there," Katie said, pointing across the campsite. I turned my head and saw a woman whose eyes were wide as saucers, muttering to herself as she pointed at Katie. "I think she sees me."

"Maybe she knows about magical creatures," I said, walking toward the woman.

"That's just old Greta," the man called after us. "Ain't nobody understands what she says, honestly. Most of us just lucky we aren't like her."

There seemed to be a hierarchy of pity even in the homeless camp, and Greta ranked toward the bottom. However, she was the only person who looked like she could see Katie, and since the only people who could see Katie were either me, Samantha, and other witches, it was a good bet that she was a witch.

"Excuse me, Greta?" I waved as I walked toward her.

"Did you know you got a ghost next to you?" Greta asked me in a soft, raspy voice.

I gestured to Katie. "This is my friend, Katie. She's nice. You don't have to be afraid of her."

"Hello!" Katie said with a smile.

"Oh hello, ghost child," Greta replied. "Such a shame when they take one so young. My apologies to your family."

"That's very nice of you," Katie said. "You're the first witch I've met who has said anything nice about my death. Most of them don't even acknowledge it."

"Excuse me? Witch?"

"You are a witch, right?" I asked. "Only witches have been able to see ghosts."

She scratched her head. "I don't know. I just knocked my head really hard one day, and afterwards of it I could see 'em everywhere. People think I'm talking to nobody, but I'm not. I can see 'em plain as day."

"I didn't think there were any left on Earth."

Greta shook her head. "There aren't many, and those that are…they're miserable. They want to go back home, but they just can't. It's a horrible life, being a ghost on Earth. Makes my life seem almost bearable. They just walk around, moping, trying to get somebody to pay attention to them," Greta turned to Katie. "You're lucky you have a human that cares. Most people don't."

Katie looked over at me. "I am very lucky. Trust me, I know."

"Don't you forget it," I said.

"Yes, we are both lucky, but I'm hoping you can help us be even luckier. We're looking for a troll, a real one. A good, old fashioned magical troll. Have you seen one?"

Greta scratched her head again. "I hear people talking a lot about a nasty bugger that lives in the sewers about a hundred meters down. Don't know if it's a troll, but nobody who goes down there ever comes up again."

"Nobody?" Katie asked.

Greta smiled. "Nah. I'm only foolin'. Some of 'em come out, but not nearly enough. Of course, not like a lot of people come looking for us, either. There's a reason we're homeless, ain't there?"

"Thank you," I said to Greta before turning to Katie. "I guess we go down the disgusting sewer tunnel."

"Yet another moment when I'm glad to be dead," Katie said. "I don't envy the smells and things you will touch."

Chapter 30

Do I really need to say how nasty that sewer pit was? It smelled like the rotten, putrid, disgusting socks you haven't washed in months mated with the rancid fish sandwich you forgot to throw away, and their power of stank fused into the most wretched smell imaginable.

The walls of the sewer pipe were lined with actual shit, or maybe it was grime, but it smelled like feces. A small creek of vile bilious sludge snaked through the base of the sewer and out into the water outside. I felt bad for any fish who swam by, minding their own business, being a fish, only to be smacked with a grotesque sludge from the literal bowels of humanity. Poor fish.

"Does it smell as bad as it looks?" Katie asked, eyeing the walls.

"Oh no," I said, trying to hold my breath. "It smells much worse than it looks."

"That's impossible."

"And yet, it's still true." I heard a crunching sound coming from further down the sewer. "Go scout ahead and see what's making that sound."

"Do I have to?"

"Yes, because you can't die again, but I can."

"Fine."

Katie flew ahead, while I crept slowly through the sewer, trying my best not to step in the sludge. "You're not going to like it," she said as she floated back to me. "Or maybe you will. I'm not sure. I mean, the troll is up there, but he's uglier and meaner than I expected."

"How ugly and mean did you think it would be?"

"Pretty ugly and very mean. But the troll looks worse than that. It's horrendously ugly and viciously mean. I think it was gnawing on the leg of a hobo. You should go back."

I pressed forward, through Katie's strenuous objections and outstretched hands. "We can't. We need troll mucus, and unless you know somewhere else where we can get any, this is our best bet."

"I can hear you, bobbin," a dark, growling voice said from further down in the tunnel. "You are coming close to me." Two red eyes shined out from the dark. "Come closer, bobbin. Let me look at you."

"I didn't come here to fight you, troll." I gulped loudly. "I come in peace."

"Well that's a shame, bobbin. Because I don't do peace."

The red eyes vanished and then a great quake in the tunnel knocked me to the ground, directly into the sewer sludge I was trying to avoid. When the ground stopped vibrating, the troll stepped out into the light. He was nearly as tall and round as the pipe itself. Red eyes glared at me above a hooked nose covered in pimples, and his yellowed teeth protruded from thick lips and scraped against his meaty neck.

The troll's massive arms hung low below his waist and his fat belly jiggled with every move, but I could tell he was strong, very strong, underneath the layers of fat on his bare, hairy chest.

"What do you want, bobbin?"

"Just a small request," I said, my voice shaking. "A bit of mucus from your snout."

The troll chuckled. "That is a very gross request, little bobbin."

"What is a bobbin?" I asked, trying to buy myself as much time as possible to scoot myself out of the pipe.

"A bobbin's a young witch, one who hasn't done her first spell. A young, fresh, little bobbin."

"I'm not a witch." I took another step backward, hoping I was being inconspicuous.

"Only a witch would want my mucus, for some witch potion or another. Ah, you're just a little bobbin though. Can't even defend herself, can you? It's barely a fair fight."

"Move, Banana," Katie said behind me, trying to block me from the troll.

"Yer familiar can't help you, bobbin." The troll took a lumbering step forward. "I can tell she doesn't even know how powerful she really is, let alone how to use that power."

"Stay back," Katie said, staying between us as best she could. "This girl isn't even a bobbin. She's very powerful. She caught a goblin just yesterday."

"A goblin, did she? That's not very impressive. It's like saying she caught a flea. There's nothing to catching goblins. Witches been doing it for ages."

I pushed myself to my feet. I could see the edge of the pipe behind me. "It's almost daybreak, troll. And I'm about to step into the light."

"You don't know how quick I can be, bobbin."

I gulped loudly. "I'm very small, and not a good meal. There must be something you desire. Anything in the world. If you let me go, I will bring it to you."

The troll stopped moving forward. "That's an interesting proposition. I always wanted to try unicorn. You ever had unicorn, bobbin? I hear it's delicious."

"Is that what you want?" I said. "I will find it and bring it to you."

The troll laughed. "What kind of bobbin, are you? Unicorns ain't real. You should know that, if you plan to be a witch."

"I must be light on my studies."

"I like you, bobbin. All right. I'll tell you what. If you bring me back a dragon heart, I'll give you mucus for whatever disgusting spell your heart desires."

I nodded. "Thank you."

"But don't come back without it, you hear?"

"We won't."

"I'll wait for you here tomorrow at sunset. Bring it then, or I'll have to eat another one of those homeless out there. They're gamey and taste like old feet, but they keep me nourished and nobody asks questions."

"We'll be back by tomorrow night," Katie said. "You can count on it."

"Well then, I suppose we have an accord."

Chapter 31

It was well after dawn by the time I returned back home. I parked Samantha's car around the block and walked to my house. I didn't want anybody to get suspicious about where I got the car. It was bad enough that I was out all night.

When I opened the front door, Mom and Joanne were sitting at the kitchen table. Their necks whipped around when they heard the door creak open.

"Oh, thank god!" Mom shouted, running toward me. She wrapped her arms around me, and Joanne was close behind. "I thought I lost you."

"I'm fine, Mom." I struggled to breath with Mom's arms so tight around me. "Can you let me go, though?"

She took a step back without letting me go and studied my face. "Where have you been? We were so worried."

"Just…out. I'm sorry I didn't call."

"I left you four messages."

"Yeah, I, uh, left my phone in the car so I wouldn't lose it."

"What car?" But I couldn't answer, so I just stared at her, stone faced. "Was it Samantha's car? Do you know where she is?"

"How do you know Samantha?" I asked, confused.

"Her mother called here last night, looking for her," Joanne said. "Frantic. We've been up all night worried sick."

I pushed away from Mom. "I'm sorry for worrying you, but I'm fine. Really."

"Do you know where Samantha is?" she asked.

I was sick of lying to my mother. I didn't know how much longer I could keep it up, so I decided to trust that she was on my side.

"Yes," I said.

"What are you doing?" Katie said to me. "They're going to think you're crazy."

"I don't care," I said, under my breath. "I'm sick of lying to everybody."

"Who are you talking to?" Mom asked, frowning.

I grabbed her tenderly around the wrists. "Mom, I'm going to tell you the truth, and I really hope you believe me."

"Of course I'll believe you. I'll always believe you if you tell the truth."

I didn't know if I believed that, but there wasn't a choice. The rift was widening every single day and soon I might need her help, or worse, she might see the rift for herself and have a heart attack.

So, I told her everything. I told her about Katie, and the Dark Place, and Samantha, about trolls, and goblins, and witches. Mom and Joanne stared blankly while I talked. I hoped they would react, or gasp, but they made no expression. When I was finished, I stared at them in silence until Joanne broke out in tears.

"I'm sorry," I said to her. "Katie and I didn't want to upset you, but you need to know. She's here and she loves you."

"Stop." Mom held up her hand. "Don't you see how much you're hurting her?" She put her hand around Joanne's. "There, there."

I took a step forward. "I'm sorry, but it's the truth."

Mom glared at me. "It's not the truth. It's some version of the truth that you concocted in your head, but there is no such thing as ghosts, or the Dark Place, or witches. All of this is just a figment of your imagination."

"I told you they'd never believe you!" Katie shouted, nearly in tears herself. "Look what you did to my mother. This is why I didn't want to tell her!"

"I didn't do anything. I just told the truth. Tell her! Just show her!"

"I can't!" Katie said. "Frank drained my power when he took my ectoplasm. I couldn't show her if I wanted to show her."

"The rift," I said. "Let's show her the rift."

"Who are you talking to?" Mom asked.

"Please, Mom. Come with me. I can explain everything. Please, if you ever trusted me before, trust me now."

Mom looked over at Joanne. "Are you going to be all right here?"

Joanne nodded. "Yes, it's just a lot. Go, go."

"I'm staying here, with my mom," Katie said.

"No, I need you with me," I said.

"You can handle this on your own. It's a big rift with ghosts and fire. If she can't see it, she's blind."

I held Mom's hand as we walked through the woods. She didn't say much, but I could tell her mind was rolling at a million miles a minute.

"This is going to prove it. You'll see."

I pulled her forward, until we reached the clearing with the hole inside of it. Ghosts were pouring from it and blue fire shot out from where it ripped open the sky.

"See!" I said, pointing at the rift.

But I could see in her eyes that she couldn't see anything. There was no wonder of fear in her eyes, just pain and sadness.

"Oh, Anna," she said, turning to me with tears in her eyes. "Don't worry. We'll get you the help you need."

Chapter 32

"I'm not crazy," I said, sitting across from Doctor Rachel in her office. My mother had driven me to an emergency appointment the morning after my "breakdown".

"I never said you were crazy." Doctor Rachel didn't look up from her notepad, where she was writing notes. "I think you're in pain though, and the type of pain you've experienced could cause any number of things."

"Just ask Frank. He'll tell you."

Rachel flipped through her notes. "Ah yes, the owner of The Witch's Brew, right?"

I nodded furiously. "That's right. He'll tell you everything."

Doctor Rachel placed down her pen. "But we did talk to him, Anna, and he told me he's never heard of you."

"That's impossible."

"What's more impossible?" Doctor Rachel said, leaning in. "That there is a world of magic that nobody else sees but you, or that you've been suffering from a bit of delusion?"

"I don't know what it says to you, but I know what I saw."

Doctor Rachel sighed. "Everybody thinks their reality is the right one, but nobody else in your life has seen these things. You realize that, don't you?"

"Katie has. Samantha has."

"Yes," Doctor Rachel said. "Samantha. Do you know where she is, Anna?"

"Of course I don't. If I knew where she was, I would tell you. If I knew where she was, I would go save her myself."

"This…Hilda, the one who abducted her. You said you saw her in the diner?"

"We talked to her in the diner."

"And the next day she abducted your friend?"

"That's what I've been trying to tell you."

Doctor Rachel paused for a moment. It looked like she was gathering her thoughts. "You know this is a safe space, right?"

I scoffed. "That's what you say, yeah? I'm not sure I agree, though."

"Well, there are some exceptions to that rule. When I think somebody might be a danger to themselves or others, or if I think they might have information pertinent to an ongoing investigation, then I have a duty to call the police."

"Okay," I said. "And why are you telling me this?"

Katie flew inside the room before she could answer. "She's saying it because there are two police officers here who are going to escort you to the station for questioning."

"What!" I said, turning to Doctor Rachel. "You're having me arrested?"

"Not arrested," Doctor Rachel replied. "Just evaluated, and the police want to ask you about Samantha. Maybe you can help them track her down."

"Some safe space this is," I spat. "I thought you cared about me."

"Sometimes the people who care about you do things for your own good, even if you don't think they are right."

I stood up. "Whatever. This is stupid."

"I told you not to tell them," Katie said as I walked out of the room.

"I should have listened to you," I told her.

"You should always listen to me," Katie said. "I give the best advice."

"Anna," Doctor Rachel said, watching me. "I hope they find your friend."

"No," I paused at the door and looked at her. "You don't. If you did, you would have just let me go. I'm the only one who can find her."

Chapter 33

"How long are you going to keep me here?" I asked the officer who had been taking my statement for the last several hours.

"Until the things you're saying start to make sense to me," the officer replied.

He was snarky, very snarky, and vain. Every few seconds he caught a glimpse of himself in the reflection of his computer monitor and smiled at his reflection. He wasn't a bad-looking man, really, and his muscles rippled through his shirt. However, his vanity made him disgusting and his lack of respect for me made him horrible.

I shifted in my seat. "I'm just going to repeat the same thing a dozen times because it's the truth."

"I've been doing this job for ten years, and one thing is always true. Eventually the fantasy washes away and people tell the truth. All of the things you've told us mean something, but until you stop living in your head and give us the cold hard facts of the case, you aren't going anywhere."

"Are you going to arrest me?" I asked. "For making up a story?"

"No, but I could for impeding a police investigation."

I crossed my arms. "Then do it already. I watch enough cop shows to know that you can't hold me more than forty-eight hours without charging me with a crime."

Officer Krupke scoffed. That wasn't his name. His name was Knutsen, but I couldn't remember that, and that song from *West Side Story* had been playing through my head ever since he introduced himself to me. He wasn't one to believe magic existed in the world, clearly. If he did, I would have gotten through to him by now.

"Just lie," Katie said, next to me. She had come with her mother to the police station. It didn't matter that Joanne couldn't see her. What mattered was that Katie watched over her.

"If I lie then it's not the truth," I thought to Katie. I agreed to let her in my head when they loaded me into the car. "If they find Samantha, they'll know I'm lying and then I'll be in trouble."

"They'll never find Samantha, Banana. We have to do that, and we can't do it if you're locked in a police station."

"We're going over this again," Officer Krupke said to me. "Start at the beginning."

I looked over at Katie, and she nodded at me. "Samantha and I went into the woods near my house to catch a goblin."

"And you're sure it was a goblin?"

I looked over at Katie again and she mouthed the word "LIE" as overexaggerated as she could with her lips.

My head dropped. "No, sir. It wasn't a goblin."

Officer Krupke leaned forward. "Now we're getting somewhere. What was it then?"

I hesitated. It made it seem dramatic but really, I was trying to come up with something feasible. "We were chasing badgers."

"Badgers are dangerous, you know? And they're not even native to this part of the country. Why would you go chasing them?"

"Samantha had a pellet gun. We wanted to hunt one down."

"Do you have a license for that?"

"No, sir. That's why I was lying. Neither of us have licenses."

"I see. Hunting without a license could be a hefty fine. You know that, right?"

"Yes, sir, but we were only playing. And we didn't find one, anyway, but we got lost deep in the woods, and that's when we saw her."

"This…Hilda person?"

"She was hideous and screaming at us. Samantha tried to defend us, but Hilda was too quick. Samantha told me to run, and I did. I'm sorry to say I ran all the way home. That is my great shame."

"Well, I have to say, that is a lot more believable than your last story, and it gives us something to go on at least."

I looked down at the floor. "Can I go now?"

The officer looked at me for a few moments. "I suppose so. Don't go far though. These missing person's cases sometimes take a while to solve, and we have a pretty terrible head start thanks to you."

"I was just trying to protect myself, and my friend."

"Well, you didn't do either very well, now did you?"

"I guess not."

Mom met me at the entrance to the police station with Joanne. Their worry for me had subsided, and now they just looked tired.

"What did they say?" Mom asked.

"They told me not to go far in case they need my help again."

"Well, that shouldn't be hard, since you're grounded for the rest of eternity."

"Can we just go home now, please?"

I felt betrayed by my mother in a way I never had before. All I wanted was to tell her the truth and have her believe me. Now, I had lied to the police and made my mother believe I was crazy. I could never trust anybody ever again, at least not until I found Samantha and put this whole matter behind us.

Chapter 34

"Why do you think Mom couldn't see the rift?" I asked, sitting on my bed after Mom brought me home from the police station.

"I don't know," Katie said. "Why did you tell her? Why did you upset my mom like that?"

"I thought they should know, Katie. I mean, I've been acting really strange, and I thought they would like to know that I wasn't crazy."

"There's a reason that I didn't show myself to my mother, or yours. I didn't think they could handle it."

"And now we know you were right."

"I guess so," Katie said. "I kind of hoped I was wrong. I really wanted Mom to see me so I could tell her that I was okay, and that I still loved her. I guess we can't do that now."

I stood up and looked out the window. "The sun's down. We promised the troll we would bring him back a dragon's heart by now, and we haven't even started."

"You can't still be talking about that with everything that happened today."

I looked over at the woods, where the rift was growing bigger with every second. "It doesn't matter what happens to me. If we don't close the puncture, then the whole world is in trouble."

"What are you going to do? You don't have a car."

I looked down at Joanne's house. Her Ford Focus was parked in the driveway. "I'm going to steal your mom's keys, I guess, since the police impounded Samantha's car."

"My mom's going to hate you for that," I said.

"Hopefully she'll understand one day. The fate of the world is in the balance."

Mom couldn't call off work, so Joanne agreed to watch me, as if I was a child. Neither of them trusted me anymore, and I couldn't say I blamed them. If I weren't me, I'd probably wouldn't have believed me, either. Besides, I was about to do something very untrustworthy.

I snuck downstairs. The television blared, and Joanne was asleep in front of *Game of Thrones*. I tiptoed across the floor to the kitchen table, where she left her purse. It wasn't long before I cupped the keys in my hand.

Not long ago the thought of stealing Joanne's car would have been appalling to me. How quickly things changed in my life once magic was introduced to it. In movies, magic always made things better, at least in the end, but in my minimal experience it turned everything pear shaped.

With the keys in my hand, I pushed open the door and snuck out into the night. As I crossed the street a lump formed in my throat. Once I stole Joanne's car, I could not take it back. It was a bond of trust that might never be repaired. However, the rift to the Dark Place loomed over our street, and I had to fix it, even if it meant destroying every relationship I had in the process.

The key slid into the door and then the ignition. It was that easy. I took one last look at my house, and then pulled out of the driveway. Soon, Joanne would wake up, and I would be in trouble. I just hoped I could get back before she found out I had betrayed her.

I looked into the rearview mirror and watched Katie float out of my bedroom window and down into the passenger's seat of the car.

"That wasn't so hard," she said, settling next to me.

"For you, maybe," I said with a chuckle. "Let's go."

I couldn't drive down to Coronado without a dragon heart, and there was only one place in town where I could hope to get one. Luckily, the Witch's Brew was open late, and Frank was behind the counter when I pushed open the door.

"You're back!" he said. "I thought the troll might have gotten you."

"Why did you lie to the police and say you didn't know me?"

"Please," Frank smirked. "First off, how do you think it would look for a grown man to hang out with a little girl."

"She's not little," Katie said. "She's a teenager."

"Even worse. Second of all, do you think they would believe me if I told them the truth? I mean, how did the truth go for you?"

"They threatened to lock me up," I said with a sigh.

"Exactly," Frank said. "And I cannot take jail. You're young and pretty. They gave you the benefit of the doubt, just like they did to Ted Bundy. Me, on the other hand, well…they wouldn't even need a good reason to lock me up and throw away the key."

"I mean, he makes a point, Banana," Katie said.

"Sure he does," I growled at her. "But I don't have to like it."

"You don't have to like anything about life," Frank said. "You just have to understand how it works if you want to survive."

"Why couldn't my mother see the rift to the Dark Place?"

"You don't know?" Frank said. "Regular people can't see ghosts. Only witches can do that."

"But I'm not a witch."

Frank chuckled. "I can tell a witch when I see one, and I smell old magic all over you."

"But my mom can't see Katie."

Frank shrugged. "Maybe it was your dad."

"No way," Katie said.

"Way," Frank said.

"If he was a witch, why did he go to war? Why did he die in that blast in Kabul?"

"We're powerful, honey, but we're not immortal and we still need money. We can't cure cancer. We can't stop old age. All we can do is delay it. Life is still life, and death is still death."

"I never saw him cast any spells."

"Maybe he had latent powers. It happens all the time. And if he was a witch, that makes you a witch, which means you can take on Hilda, and the whole council. You can save your friend."

"If I'm a witch, why didn't Hilda say anything about it when I saw her?"

"Hilda's powerful, but she's far from perfect. She only sees what she wants to see. Your friend's soul glows hot with magic, but you…you have the tiniest spark I've ever seen. Still, it's there."

"I can't think about that now. Right now, we have to close the rift to the Dark Place."

"Right," Frank said. "Did you find the troll mucus?"

I shook my head. "No. The troll told me he wanted to try a dragon heart, and if I brought him one, then he would give me some of his mucus."

Frank shook his head. "Dragons don't give them easily. Every dragon has six hearts and can only part with three to live. There are no dragon hearts from dead dragons which haven't been used to give witches and warlocks incredible strength. He's given you an impossible task."

"Maybe not," Katie said, her eyes shining brightly. "I have a plan, but it will take some trickery."

I turned to her. "Well, that seems to be our MO now, so what do you have?"

"Do you have any lizard hearts by chance?" Katie asked Frank.

Frank smiled. "I do indeed."

Chapter 35

Katie's plan involved taking a lizard's heart and expanding it to the size of a dragon's through illusion magic. Her reasoning was that dragons were basically big lizards, and that one lizard heart probably tasted like any other. I wasn't a fan of the plan, but it was the best one we had, so I went with it. The final product sat in a plastic bag beside me on the passenger's seat as I drove down to the Coronado Bridge in the dead of night.

"What do you think a dragon heart tastes like?" Katie asked, hovering over the back seat.

"Mom's had chicken heart before," I replied. "She said they're not as bad as you would think, but she wouldn't recommend them."

"They eat beef heart as a delicacy in Peru. I hear it's tender and juicy."

"Who told you that?"

"I watched a lot of TV when I was sick, Anna, especially Food Network. I couldn't eat most of those foods, so I ate vicariously through the hosts."

"I bet it tastes magical," I said. "I mean, dragons are like pure magic right?"

"So are trolls. Does that mean a troll heart tastes magical, too? What does magical even mean? Is it like cumin?"

Red and blue police lights flashed behind me. "Crap."

Katie looked back. "I told you that it was illegal to go too slow! Now what are you going to do?"

My heart pounded in my chest at a thousand beats a minute. I looked back at the police cruiser behind me. What would I tell the officer about the stolen car? What about the lizard heart in my passenger's seat?

"Come on, move," I muttered.

And just like that, it did. The police cruiser pulled into the next lane over and sped past us into the night. I had dodged a bullet, and for the first time all day I thought that fate might be on my side.

There were no more incidents before we reached the Coronado Bridge. We parked and walked down to the homeless encampment just as the sun was starting to peek out over the horizon.

"We're too late," I said.

"Maybe he waited for us," Katie replied.

I walked through the encampment but did not see Greta. Fear gripped me as I imagined that she was the one caught by the troll, and we had condemned her to being eaten by the monster. I crawled into the pipe and stood up. Even though I was more worried about Greta than I was about being drenched in disgusting sewer water, it still was none too pleasant walking through the sewer a second time.

"You're late," I heard the troll grumble from the darkness. "I was just about to eat dinner." The troll walked into the last vestiges of the moonlight, which revealed him holding Greta in his massive arms. Her mouth was covered by his huge hands, but her eyes bulged with fear. "Did you bring it?"

I nodded. "We brought what you asked for. Let her go."

"Not yet, bobbin. First, hand it to me."

"That wasn't the deal. A dragon heart for your mucus. We exchange at the same time."

"And what are you gonna hold it in, ay? Your hands? You hand me the dragon heart in that bag, and I'll spit into it. Once I have it, I'll let the woman go, too. After all, you humans taste disgusting, and this one is covered in filth."

I looked over at Katie and could tell she didn't like this plan any more than I did, but we were walking a fine line. It was barely possible to get out of the tunnel with our lives, let alone without getting eaten as well.

"Fine," I said, pulling the heart out of the bag and holding it up.

"Yeah." The troll took a step forward to look at the heart. "That's a mighty fine specimen, ain't it?"

He dropped Greta, who ran past us out of the sewer. Then, he leaned down and hocked a loogie into the bag. It was yellow and nasty. It almost filled the bag when I zipped it shut.

"Thank you."

"That should be enough, ay?" The troll said, grabbing the heart.

"Yes, this should be plenty, I think."

The troll took a big bite of the heart. Blood dripped down the sides of his mouth as he chewed loudly. "Ah, this is heavenly. You know, I never had dragon before, but if I had to guess, this would have been what it tasted like. Tender and very juicy. What a delicious treat."

"I'm glad you approve."

The troll took another bite. "Tell me, what kind of spell are you trying to bind with my mucus, bobbin?"

"There is a hole in the fabric of the universe between Earth and the Dark Place. Your mucus will help make a glue that will bind the universe back together."

"Huh. That's not what I expected. I figured you were trying to dye your hair, or something easy. So, you'll need some goblin bones, troll mucus, and dragon fire, ay? Well, and the enchantment of course."

"Enchantment?" Katie asked.

"Duh. The enchantment pulls the universe back together and then the glue binds it together again. This your first time saving the world? Of course it is. You're just a bobbin."

"Where do you get this enchantment?" I asked. "Nobody ever told us about any enchantment."

"Well, you'll need that, and the Council keeps it locked up, of course. They keep all enchantments at the Central Branch."

"Where is that?" Katie asked.

"Balboa Park, of course. You never been to the central branch? What kind of witches are you?"

"Not very good ones, it would seem. Thank you."

"No, thank you, bobbin. You done right by me." The troll took a final bite of the heart. "Just sublime."

We turned and walked away, happy that our subterfuge worked, and that we were able to live to see the next part of the tale. Of course, that was only if my mother and Joanne didn't kill me first.

Chapter 36

Mom's car was not in the driveway when I got home, which meant she wasn't home from work yet. I left the car just how I'd found it in the driveway then snuck back into the house. Joanne was still passed out on the couch as I placed the keys back into her purse and tiptoed upstairs to my room.

"Do you think you can do bad things for good reasons and still be a good person?" I asked Katie as I flopped back on my bed.

"Yes."

"No hemming or hawing about that?"

She shook her head. "None at all. Basically, every movie ever made is about people doing bad things for good reasons, and we say they are heroes. Why would this be any different?"

"Because it feels different in the pit of my stomach."

Katie floated down next to me. She placed her hands over mine. I could feel the cold from her hands on them. "That doesn't mean it's not right. We're going to save the world, okay? That's worth just about any price."

I heard Mom's car alarm beep, and that meant she was home. I listened for her to come into the house and up the stairs. Before she turned into her room, she looked into mine. When she saw I was awake, she gingerly stepped inside.

"I half-expected for you to sneak away in the night."

If I trusted her, I would have told the truth. "You don't think very highly of me."

She sat down on the edge of my bed. "Well, you're not giving me much of a reason to trust you these days."

I sat up to meet her eyes. "I thought you would have my back, no matter what."

"Just because I'm doing something you don't agree with doesn't mean I don't have your back."

I leaned forward, resting my elbows on my knees. "Doctor Rachel said something just like that to me. But I don't think you know what it means."

Katie vanished through the door. She could see it was a private moment, and I appreciated her letting me have space to talk to my mother alone.

"Of course I do."

"Then why is it a one-way street? How come when I do something you don't like, it automatically means I'm doing something wrong? What if what I'm doing means I have your back, too?"

Mom put her hand on my shoulder. "When you're an adult, you're going to have to make a lot of choices. Some of them will be good. Some will be bad. You just hope you make the right ones more than not. I know you're mad at me, but that doesn't mean I don't love you."

"You didn't answer my question."

She kissed my forehead. "I know, my love. Now, get ready for school."

I had no interest in going to school, but I didn't have a car and the school buses went all over town. After school I could take one right to the Witch's Brew to meet up with Frank after school. I had to give him the troll mucus and tell him about the enchantment.

I wrapped the troll mucus in a second and third Ziploc bag and took it on the bus. I'd had a lot on my plate over the last few days, but nothing was more stressful than when you have a disgusting bag of mucus in your bag ready to blow.

It was weird, because once I had hated Samantha for taking Katie's seat, but now, watching it empty, I missed her there. She was a good friend, and I had to get her back. I needed to save the world first, though. That was the first priority.

"Hello," I heard from the front of the class. I looked up to see Samantha standing rigidly at the front of the class. "Pardon my absence. I have been away for a few days."

The teacher smiled at her and Samantha walked to her seat. I had never been so relieved in my life.

"Samantha!" I hissed. "When did you get released?"

"Silly," Samantha said, sitting down. "I was simply away for a few days. My mother cleared it all up with the police. Now, I am here, and everything is okay again."

"Whatever," I said. "We have so much to tell you."

"I'm sorry, fellow student, but I do not know what you're talking about."

Katie and I exchanged a look and I said, "Yup, she's definitely not okay."

Chapter 37

I tried to catch up with Samantha after class, but she blew out of the room so fast I couldn't keep up with her. I finally managed to track her down at lunch, where she sat in the furthest corner of the cafeteria, staring off into space.

"What's up with you?" Katie said as she floated toward her. Samantha didn't answer.

"Hello?" I said, sitting down across from her. "Didn't you hear her?"

"Hear who?" Samantha asked. "The first thing I've heard since I sat down is you, besides the mumbling of the people in the cafeteria. They really have the loveliest conversations."

"Now I know something is wrong with you," Katie said. "You haven't thought anything was lovely since I've met you."

Samantha didn't respond to Katie at all. She just stared out at the cafeteria with a blank look in her eyes.

"She can't hear you," I thought to Katie. "Something is wrong."

"Duuuuh," Katie shot back, rolling her eyes.

"Samantha," I asked. "Do you remember us being friends?"

"I wouldn't say we're friends, but I do find you tolerable."

"At least that half sounded like you. We're going to the Witch's Brew after school today. Do you want to come with us?"

"Sounds like a silly place." She paused. "Sure."

"Great. We'll meet at your car after school."

Samantha shook her head. "My mother didn't think it was safe for me to drive myself, so I took the bus to school."

"Awesome," I said. "Meet me by the pole outside the front door after school and we'll go together, okay?"

She nodded her head in agreement and then looked off into space. Katie signaled me to follow her, and she led me into my sanctuary in the second-floor bathroom.

"Are you sure it's safe for her to come with us?" Katie asked. "Who knows what Hilda did to her."

"Exactly," I said. "It's exactly because we have no idea what she did to her that we need to bring her. If anybody would know what to do with her, it's Frank."

Katie shook her head. "This is a bad idea."

"Everything we do is a bad idea. What's one more bad idea stacked on top of the rest?"

"It's one more," Katie said. "Eventually it's too much and the whole thing spills over."

I placed my hands on the sides of the sink and looked at myself in the mirror. "I can't wait for this all to be over and for things to get back to normal."

My eyes caught Katie's in the mirror and I immediately regretted what I said. When this was all over, she would go back to the Dark Place and I would be stuck here without her.

"I'm sorry, I didn't mean—"

"No, it's okay."

"Have you ever thought about just staying here? Greta says she sees dead people wandering around all the time."

"It doesn't work like that, Anna. The souls who stay here, they never get to move on, ever. They're stuck here, even after everybody in their lives has died."

I turned to her. "But I'll stay, and we could haunt people together. It would be fun."

"That does sound nice, but you don't understand. When you're a ghost, you feel hollow, like you're not all there. I miss so much. I miss reaching out and touching things. I miss touching you. I miss hugging my mother. I miss so much. I couldn't imagine going through that forever, even with you by my side."

It was quiet for a moment while I stared at the floor. Finally, I whispered, "I hate this so much."

Katie looked at me, her ghost eyes brimming with tears. "Me too, but maybe one day we'll meet together, in the Dark Place, and go through the great hereafter together."

I smiled. "That sounds nice, but you know it's impossible. You'll go back, and dematerialize, forgetting all about me."

"Can we just dream, okay? For one second can we just dream?"

I nodded and took a deep breath. "Yeah, that sounds nice."

Even if Samantha was a little off, she still understood what it meant to meet at the flagpole after school, because when Katie and I left the school, she was there.

"You made it."

"This is the correct destination we agreed upon, was it not?"

"It's perfect. Come on."

I grabbed Samantha's hand and dragged her to the head of the bus line. One time, Katie and I had followed her friend Rebecca home for a slumber party back when she was in remission. It was near the Witch's Brew, so I knew if we took Bus 51, we would wind up near the store and could walk from there.

What I didn't expect was to get on the bus and see Rebecca staring at me. "What are you doing here?"

I panicked and stared through her for a moment, but I realized that she was waiting for an answer, which I had to give.

"I'm helping my new friend get home," I said, pointing to Samantha.

Rebecca scoffed. "I've seen her around, and she doesn't take this bus."

The bus driver turned around and looked at us. "Do one of you live on this route, because we don't run a taxi service."

"Yes, ma'am. My friend Samantha just had to move houses, and now she lives over on Donnelly near the strip mall. Isn't that right, Samantha?"

"Very right." Samantha gave a vacant smile. "Couldn't be righter."

"What's the house number?"

"She's not telling you, creeper," I said.

"Yeah, creeper," Samantha added.

"Just sit down," the bus driver grumbled. "I have to get home to my stories."

I plopped down with Samantha in the back of the bus, next to the big emergency exit door. Rebecca darted her eyes at me, and Katie looked back and forth between the two of us with an astonished expression. I looked over at the door and thought about pushing it open so I could avoid the awkwardness of Rebecca's gaze and this whole situation.

"Why is she so mean?" Katie asked. "She was never so mean to me."

"Things changed when you weren't around," I said. "People's true colors came out."

"I don't like that at all," Katie said, shaking her head as the bus jerked forward and we started to move.

The bus let us out a half mile from the Witch's Brew, and we headed toward the store. Samantha walked in silence, but Katie couldn't keep her mouth shut.

"So, you're saying that they weren't nice to you?" She asked. "Any of them?"

I shook my head. "They didn't like me, Katie. They liked you. Or, at least they liked you when you were winning things for them."

"I just can't believe Rebecca would act like that. I have half a mind to punch her in the nose."

"Well, good luck with that. I got used to it a long time ago."

"Is this why you didn't like hanging around me when I was with them?"

I nodded. "It was never about you, Katie. I always loved you, but your friends, they kind of sucked, and the minute shit got real, they abandoned you."

"They held a bake sale for me, and a car wash."

"Yeah, when you first got sick, but after the glamour of having a sick friend wore off, what happened then? They left, because it was easier. It would have been nice if one person knew you like I knew you, but now I'm alone."

Katie pointed to Samantha who shuffled in front of us. "Not alone. She's pretty cool."

"Well, she was pretty cool when she wasn't some weird zombie, but who knows what she is now. I guess we'll find out."

It took us fifteen minutes to walk from the bus stop to the Witch's Brew. Mom was already at work at this point. She had to cover a swing shift, and then work her normal hours, which meant I had until morning before she figured out I hadn't come home.

When we walked inside the Witch's Brew, Frank recoiled in terror. "Oh my god! Why would you bring that thing in here?"

"Do you know what's wrong with Samantha, then?"

"Of course I do," Frank said, his eyes wide. "She's a golem."

"A golem?" Katie replied.

"A being made of clay that just looks like Samantha. Put her in a rainstorm and she'll fall apart. Ugh, how did you make this?"

"We didn't make it," I said. "She came to school like this today."

"That makes sense. This is Hilda's magic, to keep Samantha's mother off the scent."

"How do you make a golem?" I asked.

"It's not very hard, as long as you have the right kind of clay and a piece of the subject's DNA. Getting those things is tricky, but once you have them, it's simple transfiguration magic."

"Hey," Katie said. "Can you tell where this golem thing was made?"

"Of course I can," Frank said with a snort. "But why?"

"If we knew where it was made, then we could backtrack and find where Hilda is right now."

"And if we find Hilda, we find Samantha."

"I like the way you think," Frank said. "Sure, I can put a locator spell on her origin. Just give me a couple of minutes to close up."

Chapter 38

After closing the shop, Frank led us into the back room and pressed his hand against the back wall. When he did, the entire room lit up green, slits of light emanating from cracks in the walls. The entire room shook and then my stomach leapt into my throat as we descended rapidly into the bowels of the store.

"You have a secret lair?" Katie asked.

"Of course," Frank replied. "The store is just the front that I show the world. What I do in the basement is for myself, and much more important."

"Hey," I said as the room lowered down. "Have you ever heard of the Central Branch of the Council's library?"

Frank nodded. "Of course. I've been trying to get a library card for years, but they keep denying me."

"Where is the library?" Katie asked.

"I don't know. My dear wife did, but Hilda swore her to secrecy. Now, come on. We're almost there."

The room slammed to a stop and I tumbled to the ground. Katie fell, too, only she dropped through the floor and quickly popped back up, looking a little embarrassed. Frank walked to the other side of the room and opened the door.

"Follow me," he said.

I grabbed Samantha's golem by the collar and pushed her through the doorway which led to a set of stairs, taking us even lower. Lanterns drilled into the rock walls of the cavern lit our path with an ominous green glow. When we reached the bottom of the stairs, Frank stood before a stone door adorned with a giant flaming eye.

Frank closed his eyes and brought his hands together at his chest. *"Emegtu Ligotiu Reanta."*

A small green light shone from the iris onto Frank's face. When it disappeared, the heavy doors slid open and we walked inside.

"Imendi!" Frank shouted, and green lights flickered on in the circular room. Shelves lining the walls were filled with jars of every type and size. Each jar held some sort of disgusting creature or body part suspended in liquid. I saw a brain, a foot, and a neck as I walked into the room with Samantha, but there were hundreds of other jars, too.

"Come," Frank said. "Place her here." He walked up a set of black marble stairs toward a black altar. He gestured for me to bring Samantha to him.

"What are you going to do to her?" I asked, moving forward cautiously.

"She will be dissolved into her components and we can use them to locate the source of her creation."

"You're going to kill her?" Katie said.

"That word implies that this golem is alive, which I assure you it isn't. It is no more sentient than a robot or a ventriloquist's dummy."

"What if you're wrong?" I asked.

"First of all, it hurts my feelings that you would think that, and second of all, if I'm wrong then nothing will happen. This spell will only deconstruct living clay, not bone and flesh."

I pushed Samantha down onto the altar. As I did, I felt carvings in the altar itself. Bones, and skulls, and monsters with a hundred eyes adorned the edifice.

"This is a pretty creepy place," Katie said.

"Only to you," Frank said. "To me, it is home, but I am quite comfortable in the darkness of my own soul. Now, you should both move back a little ways."

I didn't know why I needed to move back if the spell wouldn't hurt us, but I wasn't going to argue with the warlock who had brought us down to his weird magic dungeon filled with all kinds of monsters and their limbs.

Frank closed his eyes again and held his hands over Samantha's body. *"Onilgari Ventari Moldiniri."*

The room began to shake again, and the green lights shifted back into the walls so that the light snaked in circular shapes and down into the floor. The same grooves carved into the altar were carved around the whole room, making sinewy shapes along the rock and leading towards the altar. The light filled every crevice of the rocks until the altar glowed a bright, neon green.

"Frenili Bishna Ylirion!" Frank shouted, and the green light rose up from the altar into the ceiling and cascaded down all around us like a firework exploding in the air. I turned my eyes to avoid being blinded by the light, and when I opened them Frank remained, but Samantha's golem was no longer on the table. Instead, only two jars remained, one filled with clay and the other with a dim green light.

Frank picked up the jar of clay. "I'll keep this if you don't mind. Golem clay is very rare and exceedingly expensive."

"Do whatever you want with it," Katie said. "But what do we get?"

Frank walked over and placed the clay on the shelf behind him and then walked back up to the altar. He picked up the jar carrying the pale green light and walked it over to me. "This will guide you to your friend, when you are ready to find her."

"I'm ready now, but we have so much other work to do."

He shook his head. "I still need time to track down the dragon's fire. You take this and go save your friend. When you come back, I will have it ready."

"What if it leads us to Canada or Switzerland?" I said.

He shook his head. "No. Golems only have a range of two hundred miles from the person they are imitating. If it gets any further from the human that it's mimicking, the creature melts. So, Samantha must be close."

"Fine," I said. I took the jar of green light and placed it in my bag. After it was safe, I pulled out the bag of troll mucus. "Here. This is for you."

Frank grabbed the bag and held it up. "You put it in a plastic bag like an old sandwich?"

"That was all we had," I said, shrugging, palms up.

"Yeah," Katie added. "That was quick thinking on her part, honestly."

"Ugh, teenagers." Frank shook his head. "No respect for anything. Go along with you already. Make haste."

"We won't be long," I said

"Just be careful with that jar, okay? It's magically enchanted and doesn't come cheap."

Chapter 39

One thing I didn't plan for was how we were going to get home. There wasn't a good bus system in town, and I couldn't just call an Uber without my mother knowing I wasn't at home.

"What about Rebecca?" Katie asked. "She could drive you home."

"Are you serious?" I said. "She hates me."

"I know you aren't the best of friends, but you both knew me, and you could bond over that."

"I have never bonded with any of your friends before. Why do you think I'm going to start now?"

"Because you're desperate?"

I couldn't argue with that, which led me to follow Katie's directions to Rebecca's house. I had only been there once, but Katie hung out with Rebecca a lot of times and knew the route by heart.

Her house was big and nice, but it wasn't overly opulent like some of Katie's friends. She tended to know the who's who of Pine Nut Grove and could speak their language. I, meanwhile, needed an interpreter.

"Isn't she going to think it's weird that I know where she lives?" I said, walking up to the front door.

"You've been here before."

"Yeah, in eighth grade."

"Just knock. I'll bet you it won't be that bad."

"I'll take that bet."

I knocked on the door and after a few seconds heard footsteps walking on hardwood toward the door. Rebecca didn't open the door. Instead, a red-haired woman wearing an apron and a bright white smile answered.

"Why hello," she said. "Can I help you?"

I tried to think of the right words to say. "Yes, does Rebecca Swinton live here?"

"She does." The woman raised her eyebrows. "Do you want to speak with her?"

"Please," I said.

"Rebecca!" she shouted over her shoulder. "One of your friends is here!"

"Which one?" a voice shouted back.

"Does it matter? Just get down here. I have ten more pies to bake tonight!"

A few seconds later, Rebecca came barreling down the stairs. She wasn't in a good mood when I'd seen her earlier, and when she saw me standing at her door, her face went dark. "I thought you said it was a friend."

Her mother scoffed, walking back toward the kitchen. "Whatever. She asked for you." She called over her shoulder, "Nice to meet you!"

"What do you want?" Rebecca snapped.

"I need your help."

She rolled her eyes. "And why would I help you?"

I put my hands out in front of me, as if in offering. "Because we were both friends with Katie."

Rebecca raised her hand in the air to stop me. "Don't you dare bring that up. Besides, can't your new friend help you?"

I shook my head. "We got in a fight, and she won't give me a ride home."

"So call your mom, or an uber."

"I don't want her to know we were together. She…wouldn't approve…if you know what I mean."

Rebecca bit her lip, thinking hard for a moment. Then, she turned back to the kitchen. "Mom! I'm using the car."

Her mom's voice rang down the hallway. "Sounds good. Just don't be back too late!"

Rebecca reached over and picked up a set of keys from a bowl situated next to the door. "Come on."

Rebecca's mom had an awesomely tricked-out car. It had everything in it. There was leather and butt warmers and surround sound.

"What does your mother do?"

"She's a caterer. Good one, too."

"She'd have to be, with a car like this."

Rebecca looked over at me for a moment. "Don't think I like you because I'm doing you a favor. I don't want to get to know you or anything."

"Fine," I said. "I don't know why you hate me so much, though."

"Really?" Rebecca scoffed. "How about the fact that after Katie got sick you never talked to me once?"

There was a moment of stunned silence before I breathed the word, "What?"

"Yeah, I mean, I thought we were friends, Anna, and I was going through some stuff too. I mean, my friend was dying."

"You have a lot of nerve, calling her your friend," I said. "You never once came to see her during those last six months."

"Because it was too hard for me, okay? We didn't all live next to her. We couldn't all drop everything every day and be by her side. Some of us had a life."

"One time. You didn't see her one time during those last months. Not one of you came to see her."

Rebecca sighed. "I was a bad friend to her. I'll admit that. But you were a bad friend to me. You never once reached out after she became terminal. How do you think that made me feel, okay? We were all hurting."

Again, her words stunned me into silence. I hung my head. "I didn't think about it, honestly."

"We all lost our friend. Every single one of us, but you were the only one who wore it like a badge of honor. You told stories about her and went on about her like she was a prized pig. It was disgusting."

"What? Disgusting? At least I was there, Rebecca. At least I didn't sit on the sidelines waiting for somebody to tag me in."

"No," Rebecca said. "But admit it. A little piece of you was happy you got to keep her all to yourself. And don't lie to me, or I will drop you on the side of the road right now."

I took a deep breath. I looked back at Katie, who was sitting in the back seat, leaning forward, waiting to hear my answer. "It was more than a little bit of me. I was overjoyed to have her to myself most days."

"That's sick," Rebecca said. "We waited for you to let us in, to tell us it was okay to come see her, but you never did. Instead, you shut us out. We lost our friend."

"I lost my friend, too."

"Yeah, but we lost our friend months before she died because of you. So, if you want to know why I hate you, that's the reason. Happy now?"

I shook my head. "No. I don't know if I'll ever be happy again, honestly."

"Good. Maybe that's what you deserve."

Chapter 40

There was silence the rest of the car ride back to my house. When Rebecca finally dropped me off in the driveway, she barely rolled to a stop so I could get out before she sped off without saying goodbye. Her words had thrown me for a loop. I had always considered myself the hero in the story of Katie's death, but now I knew somebody, a group of people even, who considered me the villain.

"Don't worry about her," Katie said, floating over to me as I sat down on the ground. "She doesn't know anything."

"She's right, though," I said. "I could have done a whole lot more to get them involved in the end of your life. I could have arranged field trips to the hospital, but instead, I was so concerned with keeping you to myself that I forgot everything else."

"Hey," Katie said, sitting down with me. "She made it all about her, but it wasn't all about her. It was about me. I mean, I know that seems kind of lame to say, but I was the sick one, not her and not you, and I wanted you by my side more than anyone else."

I wrapped my arms around my knees. "Maybe she was right. I was just the one to get the dumb luck to live across from you and not have anything to do."

She shook her head. "No. You stopped your life for me. Nobody else did that. They kept on going but you were there for me. Never forget that."

I smiled. "I wish I could kiss you now."

"I wish that, too."

I pushed myself up off the ground and walked inside. I barely shut the door before Joanne ran over and hugged me. "Oh, thank god you're home. Have you seen Samantha?"

I shook my head. "No. Not since school."

"Her mother just called again. She's run off again. Principal Foster said he saw you getting on the bus with her after school."

I set my bookbag down on the counter. "All right, I do know where she is, and I can get her back, if you trust me."

Joanne held me at arm's length and gave me a sharp look. "Trust you? What have you done to earn my trust lately? The last time we talked, you told me my dead daughter was hanging around you. How do you think that made me feel, Anna?" She turned away from me and walked into the living room, pulling her hair tight against her scalp.

"I know you think I've gone crazy. Everybody thinks I've gone crazy, but if you want to get Samantha back, you need to trust me."

"I don't care about Samantha," Joanne said, shaking her head. "I care about you, Banana. What's happening to you?"

I looked her dead in the eyes. "I'm growing up, and when you grow up, there are things you have to do, whether you like them or not. My mom taught me that."

Joanne nodded. "That's true. I never thought I would bury my child, but I had to do that, whether I liked it or not."

I walked over to her. "I'm not going crazy, Joanne, and I'm not going anywhere, but you need to trust me. If you can't trust me, then what do we have?"

She studied me for a moment. "You can get her back?"

"If you give me your car, then yes."

Joanne thought for a moment. Then, she reached into her purse and handed me the keys. "Did you use my car the other night? When I got into it, I swear there was less gas than before."

"Do you really want to know the answer to that question?"

She shook her head. "I guess not."

"Tell Mom not to worry. I'll be home soon."

I ran out of the house and into Joanne's car. I pulled off my backpack and opened the jar that contained the green locator light.

"Okay, I don't know how this works, but I'm just going to trust it's going to work."

"It's going to work," Katie said. "I'm sure of it. Magic hasn't let us down yet."

"Really? Cuz I think all it's done so far is let us down."

The green light hovered into the air, and then it flew in front of us, onto the street. I pulled out of the driveway and put the car into drive. As I did, the locator light flew in front of the car. When we reached the intersection, it flew to the left and sat in the middle of the intersection. I thought a car would see it and crash, but one drove right through the intersection without stopping.

"I guess only witches can see it," Katie said.

I looked back at the hole in the universe over our street, then over to Katie. "Yeah, there's a lot of that going around."

The locator beacon led us down the main street until we turned right on a residential road with small, well-kept houses lining either side of the block. I found it hard to believe that one of the most powerful witches in the world was keeping Samantha in one of them, but then again, Frank had an entire basement in his shop that I hadn't known about. Clearly, witches could make things bigger than they appeared.

The green beacon flew into the air and landed on the roof of a light blue house with vegetation and thatch growing across the lawn.

"This must be it," I said, putting the car in park.

"Let's go," Katie said.

I pushed open the door and got out of the car. I wasn't sure what I was going to do when I found Samantha, but I figured it would come to me. Probably not the best strategy when going up against a powerful witch, especially since I was nothing but a bobbin.

I walked up to the door, but when Katie tried to join me, she bounced back toward the street. She tried again, but something blocked her from walking forward with me.

"It must be some sort of ward or something to keep out magical creatures," Katie said, touching the bubble again.

"Just stay here," I said. "I'll be out in a jiff."

"And if you're not?"

"Don't think like that."

I took a breath and knocked on the door. I didn't know what to expect. It could have been anything guarding the door, which was why it surprised me when the person who answered was a short, kindly, old lady with a thin, wrinkled smile.

"May I help you?" she asked, her aged voice straining. She was wearing a floral apron with a hundred pockets on it.

"Yes," I said. "Would you like to buy some girl scout cookies?"

"Oh my, yes," the woman replied. "Please come in."

She beckoned me inside and I entered the house. I almost did not see the sly, sinister smile she gave to Katie before she closed the door.

Chapter 41

The old woman's house was smaller on the inside than it had been on the outside, which I didn't think was possible. Her front door opened directly into the living room, decorated with flower wallpaper and a similar floral pattern for the couch. A doily sat on the coffee table, along with two coasters. There was no TV in the room, or any electronics of any kind that I could tell. Not even a radio.

"Now, what do you want, dearie?" the old woman said, shuffling off to the kitchen.

"Like I said, my troop is selling cookies."

"Sorry, what I meant was, what do you really want? I saw your locator spell above my house and felt your ghost familiar as it tried to penetrate my wards. So, please, do not patronize me."

"Fine," I replied. "I'm looking for my friend Samantha. A golem of her was made here, or at least I think it was anyway."

"Ah yes," the woman said, returning to the living room with a mug of hot chocolate. "I don't have much call to make golems nowadays. I remember her well."

"Is she still here?" I asked.

The woman sat down and placed the mug on one of the coasters. "In a fashion." She chuckled. "I'm sorry. You don't know that's funny yet."

I glared at her. "I don't have time for games."

"Don't you though?" the woman asked. "Your friend is still searching for the dragon fire you seek, so I think you have a moment or two."

"How did you know we're looking for dragon fire?"

The woman snapped her fingers and another mug of hot chocolate appeared on the other coaster. "It's written all over your face. Please sit. Your cocoa will get cold."

"I don't want to sit."

"My dear, that wasn't a request. I am just being polite about it. If you want to find your friend, you will sit down."

I walked over and sat down across from the woman. "I don't drink hot cocoa from strange women, but I will sit."

The old woman snapped her fingers and the cocoa vanished. "Fair enough. It's your loss. It's truly quite excellent."

"If you know about what we're after, do you know what we're making?"

"Of course," she said, taking a sip of cocoa. "It's the talk of the magical world. Do you know how much power it must take to cause a rip that big in the universe?"

"A lot, I guess."

"I've seen tears like this open before, but they almost always heal themselves in a matter of hours."

"If everybody knows about it, why haven't they gone to fix it yet?"

"Do you think it is that easy? There are forces in this world that work against the goodness, and fight to keep the portal open, even against every effort to close it."

"I'm going to do it. I just need dragon fire."

The old woman scoffed. "There hasn't been a dragon sighted in years, decades even. You need a live dragon to capture dragon fire, my dear. No. I think your quest is fruitless. That quest at least."

"What other quest do I have?"

"To save your friend, dear. Have you forgotten already?"

"Of course not. I just wouldn't call it a quest. More like a thing I have to do."

She leaned forward and whispered, "That's all a quest is, dearie."

"Can you help me then?"

She took a sip of her cocoa. "I wouldn't be here if I couldn't. I am somewhat of a fixer for the council, but to tell you the truth, they bore me. Unfortunately, I am bound to them until they release me."

"What are you?"

"A gnome, of course. How else would I have power to summon a golem and put your friend in my pocket dimension?"

"A pocket dimension? What is that?"

"Why, it's a dimension I keep in my pocket. I used to keep all sorts of things in there, but now it is only your friend, and some knickknacks."

"And you'll give her to me?"

"I could, but it's much more fun to watch you struggle to bring her back. Are you game?"

"Do I have a choice?"

"Not if you want your friend back."

"Then, I guess I'm game."

"Good, good. All you have to do is go into my pocket, find her, and summon me with a simple light charm."

"I don't know how to use magic."

"That's unfortunate, dear, but it's really easy. The council makes it out to be more complicated than it really is. Just hold up your hand and say 'Lithiori.'"

"*Lithiori*?"

My hand started to glow, and fire shot out of my fingertips. The woman caught the fire in her cocoa mug and snuffed it out. "Be careful with that power. You'll blow up the whole blasted place, won't you? Inside my pocket. When you find her, throw up a flare, and I will bring you back."

I stood up. "I'm ready."

The woman snapped her fingers. "Then off you go."

Suddenly I was lightheaded, and everything turned to black. My stomach rose into my mouth and it felt like I was falling a very long way in a short period of time.

"Goodbye," the woman said, as I faded out. "Hope you don't die."

Chapter 42

I awoke in a dark, damp place that I didn't recognize. The only light came from above me, where I saw a great eye peering down at me. The booming voice of the old gnome called out to me, "I forgot to tell you that nobody has escaped my pocket before. They usually just…die."

The gnome cackled as she stood up, and the whole pocket swayed and crashed with her. I pushed myself to my shaky feet and moved forward. Somewhere, in her pocket, Samantha was waiting for me.

"Samantha!" I shouted. The gnome took another step forward and the earth quaked under me. "Hello!"

"Anna?" I heard Samantha's voice.

I cupped my hands together. "Samantha? Where are you?"

"Be quiet," she said. "Otherwise, they will hear you."

"Who will hear me?"

But I didn't have to wait for Samantha's answer to find out. From every corner of the pocket, white critters with six legs, plump bellies, and big pinchers for a mouth converged on me. Dust mites don't look that horrific in a microscope, but in person, when you are their size, they are hideous and terrifying.

I spied a Lego block in the distance and ran toward it as the earth shook below me. The gnome wouldn't stop moving, and I suspected that was on purpose, to keep me off balance so I would be eaten by the mites.

"Where are you?" I shouted.

"The Lego!" Samantha called out. "On the other side of the Lego!"

I scanned the horizon and found Samantha hiding behind a blue, rectangular Lego piece with edges gnarled as if it had been chewed by a cat. The brick couldn't have been more than a half inch high in the real world, but it stood as tall as a house in the gnome's pocket dimension.

"Meet me at the top of it!" I shouted to Samantha.

Luckily, the Lego brick had been gnawed on all sides, which made it easy to climb. I latched onto the side of it and pulled myself up. Each one of the gnome's movements nearly made me lose my grip, but I was able to hang on and make it to the top.

Samantha was already at the top when I made it there. She looked haggard and thin, but she was still alive. I ran over to her and gave her a big hug. "It's so good to see you."

"Me too, but I wish it were under better circumstances."

I turned around and saw the bugs crawl from every part of the pocket toward us. "Don't worry. We're going to get out of here." I place my hand into the air. "*Lithiori.*"

Nothing happened. I tried again. "*Lithiori! Lithiori. Lithiori. Lithiori!*" Still nothing happened. "Why isn't this working?"

The great eye of the gnome looked down at me. "Oh, did I forget to mention…? You can't use magic in my pocket dimension. It's thoroughly warded until you reach the top of the pocket, where the magic leaks in again. Reach it, and I will retrieve you. Of course, the mites will prevent that."

"It's true," Samantha said. "They won't let us move away from this brick. Every time I try, they swarm me."

I shook my head. "We're going to get out of here. Trust me on that."

I didn't know why she should trust me. I didn't even trust me. However, I noticed that all the dust mites had crawled down from the lining of the pocket. They were only on the floor of the pocket, which meant if we could somehow get behind them, we could climb up the lining and escape, assuming they didn't catch us first.

"Follow me."

I leapt off the Lego brick and onto the back of one of the dust mites. As it turned to me, I leapt onto another one, and one after that, and one after that. I looked back to see Samantha doing the same and leaping from one mite to the next. When we finally reached the end of the dust mite army. I ran to the edge of the pocket and latched on tightly.

"Now what?" Samantha said, running up behind me.

"Now we climb."

"Are you crazy? They'll catch up to us. They have like a hundred more legs than us."

I latched onto the lining of the pocket. I pulled myself up one strand of cloth at a time. With every step I took I tried magic again "*Lithiori.*" And with every step, the spell failed to work. "*Lithiori.*"

The dust mites climbed onto the lining of the pocket dimension to chase after us. We weren't strong enough or fast enough to outrun them. Samantha was right, they would prevent us from escaping with everything they had, and they were much quicker than us.

"*Lithiori,*" I muttered again as the dust mites gained on us. "*Lithiori.*"

"This isn't going to work!" Samantha said as a dust mite grabbed onto her leg.

"*Lithiori*," I shouted one last time, and this time my hand exploded with fire. I aimed it down at the bug trying to eat Samantha. "*Lithiori.*"

Fire shot out of my fingertips. The bug fell off Samantha in a hail of fireworks. I aimed my hand at the bugs coming up close behind Samantha. "*Lithiori.*"

Again, the fire fell out of my hand. The edges of the pocket were catching on fire and I shouted again and again. "*Lithiori. Lithiori. Lithiori. Lithiori.*"

With every shot from my arms, the fire grew. The great eye descended on me, this time with panic in its pupil. "Stop that! You'll burn me alive!"

"Then bring us back!" I shouted.

"Ugh. Fine."

I grabbed onto Samantha and suddenly everything went black again. This time, instead of my stomach ascending into my throat, it fell to my knees, and when I could see again, I had crashed onto the coffee table in the living room. I pushed myself up and saw the gnome stomping on her apron trying to put out the fire.

"You're a rotten kid, did you know that?"

I turned around to see Samantha, dazed and hurt, but she was with us again. I grabbed her arm and ran out of the house as fast as I could. The fire from the gnome's apron leapt to the walls all around us.

"What happened?" Katie asked when we jumped in the car.

"I'll tell you on the way," I said.

"You talk," Samantha said, falling over in the back seat. "I sleep."

I smiled as I looked back at her. "Who knows the last time she slept?"

I'd done it. I'd rescued Samantha, and now it was time to save the world.

Chapter 43

"I can't go back home," Samantha said as I pulled up to her house.

"What do you mean you can't go home?" Katie replied. "Everybody is worried about you."

"If I go home, Hilda will find me and capture me again. You can't go home either, Anna. Not until this is over."

"I can't just stay gone. My mother will worry."

"If you go home, you'll be dead, and your mother will be in danger. We have to end this now."

"How?" Katie asked. "We don't know how to get dragon's fire or the enchantment to make the glue work."

"I think I can help you with that last thing. Hilda and the gnome who imprisoned me were always talking about the library in Balboa Park."

"We already looked that up," I said. "There's no public library there. A couple of research libraries, but they don't seem big enough to keep a collection of witch books."

"That's because the library is enchanted to be bigger than it seems," Samantha said. "And I know how to get in. The witch's library is inside the Museum of Man. If we hurry, we can get there right when it opens."

"I don't know," Katie said. "Going into a library full of witches, especially when one is hunting you, can't be a good idea."

"You're wrong. That's why it's the perfect idea. They expect us to run and hide, not enter the belly of the beast."

I bit my lip, worried. "This is a stupid idea, but it's also the only one we have, so okay. I'm in."

Katie sighed. "Well, I don't have corporeal form, otherwise I would smack you. However, since you're both on board with this dumb plan I guess there's nothing I can do but try to help you."

It took us nearly two hours to get to San Diego in the early morning rush hour. We arrived in Balboa Park just before the Museum of Man opened. I had been to the museum a few times before, including on a school trip in eighth grade, before Katie was diagnosed.

It was one of the last fun days we'd had together before the cancer took hold. Sure, we had our fun while she was going through chemo, but the days always had a sense of dread hanging over them.

"Do you remember coming here with Mrs. Haversock's class?" I asked Katie as I parked the car.

"Of course I do," she replied. "It was one of the better field trips I'd ever been on, even though the tour guide was incredibly dull."

"Ugh. He almost made me fall asleep standing up. I didn't even know I could do that."

Katie giggled. "Well, we'd also stayed up all night watching old movies the night before, remember?"

"You both have quite the history," Samantha said. "I have no idea what you're talking about though, so can you cut it out?"

"Sorry," I said. "I know it's rude. It's just that, if this goes well…we don't have much time left together."

"Until you die," Samantha said. "Then you have all the time in the world." Katie and I looked at each other, then back at Samantha. "What? Too morbid?"

"No," Katie said. "When you die, you lose your memories and become a big pile of mush."

Samantha frowned. "That didn't happen to you."

"Yeah, but that's because I had just died. By the time Anna dies, I'll have been in the Dark Place for decades. Who knows if I'll even remember her?"

"That's a huge bummer," Samantha said. "I was hoping to see my nana in the afterlife."

"Maybe you will," Katie said. "I mean, it's not like I know a lot about the afterlife. I don't even know why people can't see the hole to the Dark Place."

"It must be because of Hilda," Samantha said. "The council is keeping it hidden from everybody, so they can harness its power."

"Do you know why?"

Samantha shook her head. "No, but it must be for something big."

I opened the car door. "Well then, I think it's time to ruin their plans."

Chapter 44

The Museum of Man wasn't large, but it was opulent. The exterior was chiseled from white marble, and long, covered walking pathways led from the parking lot to the entrance on either side.

Samantha walked into the museum first and followed the directions to the research library. The library was lightly trafficked and small, or so it looked from the outside. Samantha was sure the witch's library extended far beyond the bounds of what was visible from the library grounds.

"Excuse me," Samantha said to an older librarian with horn-rimmed glasses. "I was hoping you could help me."

The librarian smiled at her. "I'm always happy to help an eager young mind hungry to learn."

"I'm looking to get a library card for this branch. How do I go about that?"

"Certainly. Well, first I would need to know the college or university you belong to, and then it's a simple reference check to make sure that you can check materials out of the library."

"We're not in college," I replied. "We're juniors in high school."

"I see. Well, that's okay," the woman said. "I can give you a day pass in order to explore the library, but you cannot check anything out without a proper card."

I leaned in. "What if we're not looking for that kind of library card?"

She batted her eyes at me. "I'm afraid I don't understand what you mean. We only issue one type of library card here."

"Are you sure about that?" Katie asked.

"Yes." The librarian bit her lip. "Shoot."

A slow smile spread across Samantha's face. "You can see her, then?"

The librarian sighed. "Yes, I can, and before you follow it up, yes, I also know that only witches and those attuned to the magical arts can see ghosts."

I leaned forward. "Then you know what kind of library card we're after, then."

She nodded. "I do, and I'll just need to see your seal from the Council to grant you one."

"Seal?" Samantha asked.

The librarian tittered. "Of course, we can't just grant access to any witch or warlock who comes in trying to learn spells. That would be chaos. We have the most advanced spells in the world—in many worlds, truth be told—locked behind our walls. Allowing just anybody to access them would be a catastrophe. We learned our lesson after the sinking of the Titanic. We can't let any old witch access information."

"Could we get a day pass then?" Katie asked. "We really only need one hour or so."

"I suppose I could grant you one for a few hours, as long as you leave everything as you found it."

"Of course," I said, nodding my head. "We'll leave everything in perfect order."

"Very well," the librarian said, waving her index finger in three concentric, clockwise circles. "You may enter."

The ground shook and a wooden staircase descended from the ceiling. "Don't worry. Nobody else can see this stairwell. Only those with magical aptitude can see anything." The stairwell descended to the ground and latched into place. "Up you go. Welcome to the Central Branch of the Witch's Library."

Samantha and I climbed up the staircase while Katie floated next to us. When we reached the top of the stairs, I opened the hatch and pulled myself into the library. It was a great bit of illusion magic. The witch's library seemed to extend forever, rising a hundred feet into the air. Books lined every inch of the walls, which towered further than I could see, and witches zipped across the air carrying hardbound volumes in their arms.

In front of us was another information desk like the one in the research library below, except this one was exquisitely carved wood, inlaid with silver monsters from minotaurs and hydras to dryads and pixies. The same librarian from the main library smiled at us from behind the counter.

"How may I help you?" she said.

"Didn't we just see you downstairs?"

The librarian laughed. "Another bit of illusion magic. I project a mirror version of myself to guard the entrance of the library from any who wish to do it harm."

"But that version of yourself downstairs used magic," Samantha said. "I didn't know an illusion could use magic."

"Yeah," Katie said. "Samantha's golem couldn't even see me. How could a mirror see me?"

"Because I see through my illusions' eyes and control it like a puppet. Usually, it stays silent since the research library is not well trafficked, but my mirror-self allows me to be in two places at once and use magic in both."

"Sounds complicated," Katie said, floating toward the front desk.

"Nothing simple is worth doing, familiar. Without some complications, well, life would get quite dull, wouldn't it?"

"Why does everybody call me a familiar?" she asked.

"Well, you are bound to this witch, are you not? Generally, ghosts are not allowed autonomy by their captors, and certainly do not ask questions."

"I believe in freedom," I said, joining Katie at the desk.

"That will change with age, I'm sure. You young witches do not understand the pitfalls of free will. You will, though, with time. Now, how may I help you?"

"We're looking for a book," Samantha said.

"Well, you are in the right place. We have the most books on witches and witchcraft anywhere in the world. If there is a book, then we certainly have a copy, if not the original."

"Great," I replied. "We're looking for one spell in particular."

The librarian turned to her computer and started to type. "And what kind of spell is this. Illusion? Defense? Offense? Healing?"

"Healing, I guess," Katie said.

"Would you mind very much telling your familiar to behave and stop addressing her betters?"

I looked over at her. "Cool it."

"Seriously?" Katie said.

I nodded. "Please."

"Very odd, for a familiar. You really say 'please' to it?"

I nodded. "Of course. Manners are everything, are they not?"

"Hrm," the librarian sniffed. "I suppose I can't argue there. Now, what kind of healing spell are you after?"

"One that can mend a hole between our world and the Dark Place."

"That is very advanced magic, children, and dark as the name suggests. You aren't practicing the dark arts, are you?"

Samantha shook her head. "Of course not. It was an assignment, for our teacher, Mrs…Mrs. Mogon."

"Well, your teacher has very bad luck then. I'm afraid we only have one book with the complete spell in it, and it's been checked out for quite some time."

"Only one book? But it must be a more popular spell than that," Samantha said.

"Well, I can't speak to its popularity, only to its power, and we don't make a habit of duplicating magical spells all willy-nilly. That kind of magic is kept under lock and key, away from prying eyes. Unfortunately, that means we have only had one book with the spell and the enchantment, and it's not available."

"What about just the enchantment?"

The librarian typed into her computer. "No, I'm sorry. Still only the one."

"What happened to it?" Samantha asked.

"It looks like it's been checked out for the last decade."

"It's been checked out for ten years?" I asked, exasperated. "And nobody's needed it?"

"That's correct. Oh, dear me. She will have quite the fine, yes, she will. I must get one of my new bursars to investigate. It seems like the last bursar to look into it died a horrible and unexplainable death."

"Maybe we could find it," Samantha said. "We're very good at finding things."

"I don't think that would be appropriate."

I turned to Katie and used my thoughts to tell her to look up the address. She nodded and hovered into the air. As she did, she twisted around the desk ever so slightly to get a better angle on the book. I saw her lips move as she read the address, and when she nodded slowly, I knew she had the address memorized.

"That's okay," I said. "I understand. We're sorry for wasting your time."

Chapter 45

We followed the address Katie had memorized through downtown San Diego and up into Mission Viejo. After my run-in with the gnome, I worried that following a random address in a witch's library could lead to another confrontation with a magical creature, but we needed the enchantment badly, and, as far as I knew, this was the only way to get it.

"The name of the book is called *Saving the World: Spells to Stop Doomsday*," Katie told us as we pulled into a residential neighborhood with big houses and nicer cars.

I parked on a steep incline and we walked up to the front of a house painted a muted yellow. It was more of a mansion than a house, really, being three stories tall and blanketed with ivy. The front door was covered in gold fleck, and the door knocker was the shape of a roaring lion. I pulled the door knocker back and let it go. The thunderous echo roared through the house.

The door opened almost immediately, revealing a smiling butler dressed in a tuxedo with a bow tie. "May I help you?"

"We're here…um…I don't know how to say this," Samantha said, scratching her head.

"We're here to see the lady of the house," I said. "It's about a library book which she has had on loan for some time."

The butler scoffed. "I'm afraid the lady does not have time for such trivialities."

"Who is it?" a woman's throaty voice came from the back of the house.

"Some children, ma'am, inquiring about a book," the butler replied. "Shall I send them away?"

"No, please!" I shouted into the hall behind the butler. "Listen, we really need a book you have on loan!"

A pause, then the voice replied, "Which book?"

"Saving the world!" Samantha yelled this time. "It's got all sorts of spells about preventing doomsday."

"Please," I said. "It's a matter of life and death."

There was a long silence. I expected her to tell me to piss off. After all, that's probably what I would do if a bunch of teenagers banged on my front door.

"Let them in," the voice said.

"Yes, ma'am," the butler said. He looked us over from head to toe and then added, "Please wipe your feet."

The butler led us inside the house, which was just as opulent as it was on the outside. A bejeweled chandelier hung from the center of the foyer. Long staircases covered in red carpet ascended up either side of the room and led to a golden door at the top of the staircase. In front of us, a large crystal dragon rose ten feet into the air, screaming silently into the air as we walked inside.

"Please be careful not to touch anything," the butler said. "The dowager Vermilda's collection is quite priceless."

"What is the difference between priceless and quite priceless?" Samantha asked.

The butler raised an eyebrow and said, slowly, "Several hundred million dollars."

I turned to Katie and she looked deep into my eyes, waiting for me to tell her what to do. "Search the house for the book," I thought to her, and she nodded. The butler never looked at Katie, so I was sure he wasn't magically adept. The woman we were meeting, however, was another story, and I needed Katie to disappear before we met her.

The butler led me and Samantha through the foyer and down a long hallway with gilded-framed paintings of dragons hanging on either side.

"Your boss likes dragons," Samantha said.

"She is quite taken with them, but who wouldn't be? Marvelous creatures, dragons."

I shrugged. "If you like that kind of thing. I don't suppose you know where we could find a dragon, do you?"

"They are a myth, my dear. I'm afraid just the product of overactive imaginations."

I chuckled. I wasn't sure if he was playing me or if he really didn't know anything about magic, but it seemed as though he was either naïve or stupid. It didn't matter, though, because he wasn't the person we were there to see.

The hallway opened into a pink sunroom with golden accents where each wall met the next one. More paintings of dragons covered the walls, except for the far wall which was made up of floor-to-ceiling windows. In the dead center of the room, an elegant woman dressed in a white gown puffed on a cigarette from a long cigarette holder.

She looked like the star from the golden age of cinema, the type that Katie and I used to watch. She rose from the couch and walked toward us as if she were gliding on air. She took a puff off her cigarette and blew it into the air, walking through the smoke as she came toward us.

"These are them?" she asked her butler.

"Yes, ma'am," the butler replied. "I didn't get their names as I didn't think it was very important."

"Very good, Chevrold. Away with you now." The woman flicked her wrist and the butler spun on his heels and disappeared down the hallway. "Now, who may you be?"

"I'm Anna," I said, then pointed to Samantha, "and this is Samantha."

"And who is your other friend?" she asked. "The ghost who is so rudely going through the books in my library."

"I don't know what you're talking about."

The dowager Vermilda smiled, showing her glistening teeth. I gasped in spite of myself and felt Samantha stiffen next to me. They were pointed, like a shark, instead of round. "My dear, please do not lie to me. I am more powerful than you could imagine."

The woman snapped her fingers, and Katie appeared before us, confused and frightened. "Where am I?"

"In my sunroom, my love," the woman said. "It's very rude to sneak around a person's house, don't you know that? Or did you lose your manners when you died?"

"I…I…I did, clearly."

"Well, at least you are honest. Dumb, but honest. Who are you?"

"I'm Katie."

"You're not the familiar of either of these people, that much I know for sure. Your stink is not all over them, nor theirs over you, so what do you want, ghost?"

"She wants the book, just like us," I replied.

"Let her answer," Vermilda growled.

Katie spoke up. "I want to save the world."

"Well, that is interesting." The woman walked back to her seat. "I've haven't heard that one in some time. Come, sit. Let us chat. Perhaps we can help each other."

Chapter 46

"I don't very much like magicians," the dowager Vermilda said, sitting on the lounge chair on her deck. She had Chevrold bring us lemonade and we were sitting around her patio table where we could look out on the whole valley below us.

"I don't very much like them, either," I said. "None of us do."

"Interesting." She looked me up and down. "Since you have come from the magician's library."

"Not because we wanted to. We're trying to close a portal to the underworld, and we need that book to do it."

"Ah yes, the book. But to close a portal like the one you described, you need more than just the book. You need goblin bones, troll mucus, and dragon fire, too. Of course, those ingredients can damn the world as quickly as save it."

"What do you mean?"

"Those three ingredients are the most powerful in all magicdom. Yes, they can close the portal, but they can do so much more. I hope you know what you're doing."

"We don't," Samantha said. "We're just guessing here."

Vermilda smiled again, revealing her spiked teeth. "You are brutally honest. I'll give you that. Stupid, but honest."

"We have the goblin bones and troll mucus," Samantha said, taking a sip of her lemonade. "We're just missing the dragon fire, and the enchantment."

"Well, those are the two hardest parts to come by, so you don't have very much of anything now, do you?"

"We don't, and since we're not witches, it's been very hard."

"It's very hard for anybody, even a master magician. There hasn't been a dragon sighting in a thousand years. Though, even when they were around, most thought they were more trouble than they were worth."

"We don't know anything about that," Katie said. "We just want to close the portal."

"But why, my dear? If you do that, you'll have to go back, won't you? The life of a ghost wandering Earth is a fate worse than death but returning to the Dark Place means that you will forget everything you learned here, and everyone you loved."

"At least I'll be able to save everyone I love who's still on Earth, and that means everything."

The woman smiled at Katie, revealing her sharp teeth once again. "And what do you think of that? Since you love her so. Do you want her to return home?"

I shook my head. "I don't, but she won't stay, and I won't make her."

"We talked about this," Katie said. "I can't stay."

"Yes, you could," I replied. "She just said you could."

"She said wandering Earth is a fate worse than death."

"But at least we would be together," I said, tears forming in my eyes. "Doesn't that mean anything?"

"It means everything to me, but you can't love me forever. Okay?"

"Sure I can, and I will."

"No!" Katie said. "I won't let you live in the past. I'm a ghost. You need to love the living, not the dead, okay? It would break my heart every day if you couldn't move on from me, and if I stayed here, I know you wouldn't."

"Isn't that my choice?"

She shook her head. "No, it's both of our choices."

The woman leaned forward. "I think I have a solution to your problem, Anna. You clearly love her, don't you? So much that it hurts?"

"Yes," I said, tears streaming down my face.

"And you could never imagine being without her."

"Never."

"What if I could make that all go away?"

"What do you mean?" I asked.

"First love is one of the most powerful forces on Earth. So much can be done with it. So much can be accomplished with that kind of power. If you would give it to me, I would give you the book."

"Give you…my love for Katie?" I said.

"Absolutely. Then, you can move on, and say goodbye, when the time comes."

I looked over at her. "I couldn't—"

"It's for the best," Katie said. "It gets us what we need, and you get to move on. It's win-win."

"Is that what you want?" I asked her. "Do you want me to just forget the feeling I have for you, like it never existed?"

"When I return to the Dark Place, I'm going to forget about you. And if you stop loving me, you can move on."

"I can't believe what I'm hearing," I said, shaking my head.

"Then it's even better that you give your love to her, so that I can never break your heart again."

"I need to think," I said, pushing up from the chair and running inside.

"Anna!" Katie shouted after me, but I was already through the door.

Chapter 47

"Do you have a bathroom?" I asked the butler when I saw him inside. There were tears streaming down my face.

He pointed an impassive finger down the hallway. "First door on your right."

I ran down the hall as fast as I could and slammed the door closed behind me. Like the rest of the house, it was filled with dragons, from the faucet to the painting on the wall, and every inch of the room was trimmed with gold. As I stared into the mirror, a dragon painting stared back at me.

I couldn't believe Katie. I had just gotten her back, and we had just professed our love for each other, and now she just wanted me to throw it all away and get over her. Like it was that easy to get over somebody. If you could just give your love to somebody else, wouldn't that make things too easy?

I grabbed a wad of tissue paper and blotted my red eyes. As I did, I heard a knock at the door. "Can I come in?"

It was Samantha. I ignored her but she knocked again, and then a third time. I knew I couldn't avoid answering her. "It's not really big enough for two people."

"I'll sit on the toilet, or something. Please let me in."

"Fine." I pulled open the door and Samantha squeezed inside. "I told you it was small."

"It's fine." She sat on the toilet seat. "Are you okay?"

"The love of my life just told me I should give away my love for her, as if it was just that easy."

Samantha took a deep breath. "I know this is hard to hear, but you're being a baby."

"Excuse me? I thought you were here for emotional support."

"That's never been my strong suit," she replied. "I'm very good at telling the truth, though, and the truth is we're screwed without that book."

"No. There has to be another way to get that spell."

"Before the hole opens even wider and we're all consumed by it?"

"I can't do it, Samantha. I just can't give up my love for somebody, like it's nothing."

"Who said it was nothing? I was there, too, and Katie seemed every bit as upset as you. She's just being practical. What are you going to do? Pine for a ghost your whole life?"

My eyes dropped to the sink. "Maybe just until college."

Samantha shook her head. "It's not practical or smart, Anna. You don't have to give away your memories, but don't be an idiot. You're going to move on some day. It might as well be today."

I blew my nose. "I don't want to move on. I'm not ready yet."

"Katie wants you to move on. She wants what's best for you. That's what people who love you do. They look out for you, okay?"

I spun around to catch her eyes. "Just because you're right doesn't mean I have to agree with you."

Samantha stood up and placed her hands on my shoulders. "You don't have to agree with me to do the right thing, either."

Samantha was right, but I didn't have to want her to be right. It just didn't seem like enough, to give away the love of my life for a stupid book. It didn't seem big enough, grand enough.

I looked past Samantha's head, to the dragon on the wall behind it, and then I had an idea. It wouldn't make me feel any better, but it might make it more worthwhile to give up the only love I had ever known.

I pushed open the door and walked back outside to meet the dowager. When I did, Katie turned to me. "Are you okay?"

"No, I'm horrible, but that doesn't mean I'm not going to do it."

"So, you've come to your senses," Vermilda said, taking a long drag of her cigarette. "I knew you would. They always do."

"Not so fast," I said. "Your deal isn't nearly good enough. I need more if I'm going to give away the love I feel for Katie."

"Piffle," Vermilda said, rolling her eyes to the ceiling. "I'm giving you the key to save the world. What more do you want?"

A slight grin came across my face. "I want dragon fire."

Vermilda scoffed. "Please. What makes you think I have access to dragon fire?"

"The thousand paintings of dragons in this house. Either you have it, or you know how to get it. I want the book and dragon fire, or there's no deal."

Vermilda slammed her hand on the table. It wasn't the dainty fingers of a movie star, that's for sure. Her fingers were long and scaly, with dark, black talons. "You are lucky I need your power to maintain my disguise, or I would eat you right now."

"What's going on here?" Samantha said, stepping onto the patio.

I gulped loudly. "I think we're the first people to see a dragon in over a thousand years."

"Don't get cocky," Vermilda said. "Many have seen me, just none in my true form. I haven't been able to leave the house in ages, what with my teeth like they have been. And now, it's getting worse."

"Do we have a deal, then? Since you need what I have so badly?"

"Do you have something to transport the dragon fire in? Or should I just burn you alive?"

I nodded. "I have an enchanted jar in my car."

"Then we have a deal."

I turned to Katie. "I hate that we have to do this. I was prepared to love you for the rest of my life."

"I don't want that for you. I already loved you for all of mine. I want you to find somebody, grow old, and make memories. We couldn't have done that together. The fates wouldn't allow it, but I don't want you carrying a flame for me forever."

"I hate this," I said, crying again.

"I do too," Katie replied. "But it's the right thing. The best thing for you. For us."

I moved my head closer to hers, until I could feel the cold chill from her aura on my scalp. She turned her head to the side and placed her icy lips over mine. I closed my eyes, and for a minute we were like a normal couple, and my mind raced to what we could have been if the cancer hadn't taken hold of her.

Katie pushed back. "The cancer was what brought us together," she said. "I wouldn't have changed those memories for anything. I loved more in those few months than most people do in a lifetime."

"I love you. I will always love you."

"No, you won't. That's kind of the point."

"I know, but it's just a thing to say."

"Ugh!" the dowager said. "Is this display over, yet? Can we get on with it?"

I nodded, turning to her. "Will it hurt?"

She shook her head. "No. When I'm done it will take the hurt away."

She snapped her fingers and my body became white hot. I felt something creep up my bones. My mouth opened on its own, and a stream of glittering pink light flowed out of it toward Vermilda. She opened her mouth, and the pink glitter flowed into it. As it did, her teeth turned from spiked to square, and her arm turned from a claw back into a delicate hand.

"How do you feel?" Samantha asked, as she helped me to my feet. "What do you feel?"

I looked over at Katie, and I started to cry again. This time it wasn't for what was said, but for what was lost. "Nothing. I feel nothing."

Vermilda and Katie were wrong. It wasn't better to lose the love I felt in my heart, no matter how much it hurt. It was so much worse to feel nothing.

Chapter 48

It's hard to describe the completely hollow feeling after having all the feelings you held for the love of your life sucked out of you. Every time I looked at Katie on the ride home, I felt nothing. I remembered the memory of feeling something at one point, but now there was just…nothing. When I looked back at Samantha, I felt friendship. When I looked at the road, there was fear and panic. When I looked at Katie, though, there was nothing, like wind flowing through the hole in a wooden log. I felt the emptiness as it brushed against my soul.

"Are you okay?" Katie asked. I was pulling off at the exit that led to the Witch's Brew. "You haven't talked much since we left the dragon lady."

"I'm fine," I replied. I braked at a red light. With the car stopped, I closed my eyes and took a deep breath. "No, that's not true. I'm not fine."

"What can we do?" Samantha asked.

"Let's just finish this, okay?" I pushed on the gas when the light turned green.

It hadn't been storming on the highway, but as we neared the Witch's Brew, dark storm clouds were gathering. A bolt of lightning crashed before us in the street. I swerved to avoid it, convinced that I would head straight into oncoming traffic.

But there was no traffic. None at all. In fact, I hadn't seen any cars since we exited the freeway. The lights were off in all of the houses we passed, and even the street lamps didn't flicker. There was nothing but darkness, the occasional flash of lightning, and the headlights from our car.

"This is eerie," Samantha said.

"I agree," Katie added. "I'm creeped out, and I'm a ghost."

When we reached the strip mall, we found the only store with lights on was the Witch's Brew. The door had never been locked before when we came, but when I went to turn the handle it wouldn't budge.

"Frank!" I shouted. "Let us in."

"Go away, demon!" Frank called from the other side of the door. "I won't succumb to you!"

"I'm not a demon!" I banged on the door louder.

"That's what a demon would say!"

"Just let us in!" Samantha shouted.

"Oh, so you can change voices now. Very clever."

Katie tried to move through the door to the other side, but a green forcefield bounced her back. "Ow."

"That's right, demon. You can't get in here. My ward game is powerful."

"It's not a demon. It's Anna, Katie, and Samantha."

"Prove it."

"How?"

"Tell me something only I would know."

"Um, you have a creepy elevator in the back of your store," Katie said. "And a crazy weird dungeon thing underneath your store, too."

"Yeah," I added. "It's filled with gross monsters and stuff…"

"Really?" Samantha asked. "I wish I'd seen it. It sounds awesome."

I flashed a smile. "It was kind of awesome."

There was shuffling behind the door, and then it opened to reveal Frank, pale white and shivering like he had hypothermia.

"Thank the gods it's you," he said, wrapping me in a hug.

"We're not really that kind of friends," I said.

"Sorry," he said, letting me go. "It's just been a freakshow out here since you left. Come in before something eats you."

Frank pulled Samantha and me inside and shut the door once Katie had joined us. The inside of the store looked nothing like the neat, tidy place we left. There was barbed wire laying across a metal enclosed counter, and large wands and guns pointed at the door from every angle. On the floor was more barbed wire which glowed pink and green. Frank stepped over everything carefully on his way behind the counter.

"Sorry for the mess. You know how it is."

"No, we don't. What happened here?"

Frank slammed his hands on the metal counter. "Well, I've always been prepared for the end of the world. All my cabinets and shelves have these metal barriers which can surround them the moment any danger comes my way."

Above the roof, a crow cawed, but at least a hundred times louder than I had ever heard one squawk before. "What was that?"

"Those are the murder crows, or at least that's what I'm calling them. They're fifty feet tall and armed with great black eyes which shoot magic beams out of them. Don't want to mess with the murder crows."

"What do you mean, murder crows?" Samantha said. "I haven't lived in this town for long, but I don't remember there being murder crows."

"Nor would you. This place has changed since you've been gone. Hilda came with her gaggle of witches and took over the town. They've been growing the rift bigger with each passing moment, and it's making everything go wonky."

"So murder crows came to town between the time when Hilda captured me and now?" Samantha turned to me. "Why didn't you tell me?"

"I didn't know about them." I held my hands up. "Neither did Katie. Did you?"

"Of course not. I think I would remember murderous crows that shot lasers."

"Magical beams," Frank corrected.

"Whatever," Samantha said. "Same difference."

"Yes, but lasers are science fiction, and magical beams are fantasy. And magical beams just feel right for where we are right now, with the magical murder crows and all."

I stepped toward the counter, careful to avoid the barbed wire. Frank watched me with wide eyes. "I wouldn't do that, if I were you. Those things are rigged to explode at the slightest touch."

"Fine." I took a step backwards. "Then how about you explain what happened, and just assume none of us have ever heard of murder crows."

"It was horrible. Hilda and her ilk showed up soon after you left. I tried to stop them, but they overpowered me, and I had to hole up here, hoping you would return with a solution to close the rift forever. I don't know what they have planned, but it's something big, and with the power of the Dark Place, they can basically harness unlimited magical power."

I looked at Katie and Samantha, then back to Frank. "If that's the case, then we have to stop it, now."

"Does that mean you have all the ingredients?" Frank asked. "Please tell me you found some dragon fire. All my searches have been fruitless."

"We have it," Samantha replied.

"Bring it here," he said, holding out his hand.

"First, let down your booby traps."

Frank snapped his fingers and the barbed wire on the ground disappeared. "Fine. You're no fun." I handed Frank the book and the dragon fire. He brought the dragon fire to his face and stared at it. "I've been looking for you for so long."

"Can you make the glue we need with these ingredients?"

"Of course." Frank nodded without taking his eyes off of the fire. "Just give me a few minutes and then, you'll be off to save the world."

Chapter 49

Samantha and I sat on the metal counter, which used to be glass. But that was before everything apparently went to Hell, after we left to find Samantha.

"So, you just feel nothing for her?" Samantha asked, looking over at Katie, who hovered near the door.

"Literally nothing. I mean, I've said I don't feel anything for somebody before, but I always felt something. With her, I feel nothing. Like a literal hole in my heart."

"That sucks," Samantha said.

"It does, but it also doesn't. I hate to admit it, but there's something nice about not being bitterly sad that she's going to leave back to the Dark Place when this is all over."

"That's if we win," Samantha said. "We're going up against Hilda and the whole council. Look at us. We're not qualified for that. They're going to destroy us"

"I know," I said. "But we have to win. The fate of the whole world is at stake."

"How are we going to do that?" Samantha asked. "We don't even know magic."

The back door opened, and Frank stepped out, holding a jar of white paste in his hands. "This should help." He placed the jar on the metal counter between me and Samantha. "It's a pretty good batch, if I do say so myself."

I grabbed the jar from him and studied it. "This is really going to save the world?"

Frank shrugged. "I don't know. It's supposed to, but honestly, it was never meant for this big a tear."

"It has to work," I said. "But we still have no idea how to beat Hilda."

Frank grabbed a book from the case behind him and slammed it on the counter. "My wife had this book on her when she died. It's the only one I was able to keep from her library. It's full of offensive spells which can take down a witch. Most of them take months to master. Luckily, I'm not much of a student, so I can show you the ones which take the least mana, including the power of flight."

I hopped down from the counter. "Let's do it."

Frank opened the book and held out his hands. "Okay, hold out your hands like this, like you're making a square." Each of us brought the thumb and index finger of our hands into a square. "Now, repeat the power word, *Levithian*, as you imagine yourself lifting into the air. As you say it, bring your hands to the ground and push them into the ground, like you're using your arms to push off the ground."

I made the square and closed my eyes. I felt idiotic, but I couldn't doubt myself, or Frank. He was my best chance at saving the world. "*Levithian*," I mumbled under my breath, but nothing happened. I repeated it again, but I still didn't lift off the ground.

"You're not picturing yourself light enough," Frank said. "Look at your friend. She's doing it."

I opened my eyes and saw Samantha floating in the air. She was doing it. She was really doing it, and suddenly I got very competitive. It could be done, and I was determined to do it as well.

"*Levithian*," I said, imagining myself flying through the air. "*Levithian*." I pushed my hands down to the ground and pushed off from it. My feet suddenly felt like they were disconnected from the ground. I opened my eyes, and saw that they were, because I was in the air, floating as if I were a bird.

"Whoa," I said.

"Great job," Frank said. "It took me three days to master that, and you've done it in minutes. Very impressive."

"Well, we have something to fight for," Samantha said.

"Good," Frank said. "You'll need that fire in your belly to beat Hilda. You can control your flight with your hands. So, now put them over your head and push down like you are pushing back to the ground."

I did, even though I didn't want to do so. I raised my hands into the air and pushed until I touched the ground again.

"You can only do one spell at a time," Frank said. "At least, at the level you're at right now. One day, if you're really powerful, you might be able to cast two or even three spells at the same time. For now, stick to one."

"What's next?" Samantha asked.

"Now, I show you how to shoot fire."

"Oh, I know this one," I replied. "*Lithiori.*"

A burst of fire came out of my fingers and shot through the air. Frank ducked to avoid it, and it bounced every which way, until it finally flew through Katie, where it fizzled out inside her aura.

"That was weird," Katie said, strangely calm.

"Did it hurt?" I asked.

"No," Katie said. "It kind of tickled. I think I liked it."

"Want me to do it again?" I asked.

"Please," Katie said.

"Maybe later," Frank said. "When we're not inside my very flammable store."

"Sorry," I said.

"Besides, that's not the fireball I'm thinking of. Watch."

Frank held his arms together in front of him and rotated them around like he was rubbing an imaginary beach ball.

"*Fiorini*," he whispered. A small ember of fire grew between his hands, and as he moved his hands the fire grew, and grew, and grew. "This is your best weapon against the witches. The longer you let it grow, the bigger it will get, and you can use it to blow them away. Be careful though, the bigger it gets, the more unstable, and the more mana it takes. You need to concentrate to control it, and let it go before it consumes you, or it will burn you alive."

I nodded. I placed my hands together in front of me and started to rotate them as if they were rubbing a tennis ball. "*Fiorini*." The fire started instantly, and as I massaged my fake globe, the fire grew and grew.

"Great work," Frank said. "Now, Katie, open the door."

"Um, I can't. I'm a ghost."

Frank shook his head. "I enchanted it to be felt by your aura. Try it."

Katie touched the door and it opened for her. For a moment it was like she was human again, and a great smile came across her face.

"Outside," Frank said.

I ran outside with my fireball and Samantha followed with hers. The wind howled and the sky crackled. It was dark as Vantablack. All the light came from Frank's store and the fireballs in our hands.

"To fire," Frank said, "just imagine the target and push out your arms." Frank pointed to a green dumpster next to his store. "There."

I looked over at Samantha and nodded. I pushed forward my hands and the fireball flew out of my hands and smashed into the dumpster. A couple seconds later, Samantha's fireball exploded behind mine, igniting the dumpster in a roaring fire.

"Very good," Frank said. "Now, that is all we have time to learn. Come inside and copy the enchantment. You will need it to bind the rift together while you repair it. I only hope we are not too late."

Chapter 50

Frank said his goodbyes quickly and we hopped into the car. I didn't know what we were going to do exactly, or how we were going to stop Hilda, but I figured that if we got closer to the rift, a plan would present itself, or we would die trying.

"That can't be good," Samantha said. The rift had grown considerably since we'd last seen it and was widening with each passing second.

"None of this is good," Katie said as she peered out the window.

From behind us, I heard the squawking of the murder crows. I looked in my rearview mirror and watched one of the birds flap toward us through the air.

"Um, guys." My voice almost cracked, I was so afraid. "I think you should look behind us."

Even in the seconds that it took to say those words, the enormous bird cut the distance between us in half. Samantha opened her window and hung her head outside of it.

"What are you doing?" I asked.

"Just trust me." She pushed herself out of the window until her whole torso was outside of the car. "*Fiorini.*"

"Stop!" Katie said. "Frank told us that it was unstable and dangerous!"

"Yeah," Samantha replied, "and what do you think that murder crow is? Completely stable?"

From the side of my eye I watched the fireball grow and grow. "Let it go!"

"Just a little longer."

A pickup truck was turned over on its side in the middle of the road. I swerved to miss it, and I heard an explosion underneath us. Samantha screamed.

"Stay straight! You almost killed us!"

"She's right," Katie replied. "I'm already dead, but that blast was so strong it would have killed me a second time!"

"Just keep the car straight," Samantha yelled as she went about constructing another fireball.

A lightning bolt crashed in front of us and I swerved the car with one hand while I grabbed onto Samantha's jacket with the other.

"Get inside the car!" I shouted.

Samantha hung outside the car, flailing her arms and trying to push herself back inside. If I let her go of her, she would fall out onto the road for sure, and if I slammed on my brakes to drag her inside, the murder crows chasing us would take us down. I looked quickly in the rearview mirror and saw a second crow lining up for another dive bomb at us.

I had no choice. I took my foot off the gas and pulled Samantha inside with both my hands. She huffed and puffed with all the hysteria of somebody who was just about to die.

"You nearly killed me!" she screamed.

"And I saved your life!" I snapped back, stepping harder on the gas.

"Guys!" Katie screamed.

The crows were no longer behind us. There was another crash of lightning, and then an enormous crow talon tore through the hood of our car.

All three of us shrieked when a second pair of crow talons ripped through the roof, leaving very little but a mangled sunroof for us to look out of. I pressed on the gas, trying to escape the crows, but they just flapped above us, easily keeping pace with the car.

Another lightning strike crashed into the hood of the car, electrifying the hood and sending shockwaves down the outside of the car. The car jerked to one side, and tipped over, crashing and spinning along the ground, until we skidded to a stop upside down. Luckily, I was wearing my seat belt, but the air bag deployed and slammed me right in the nose.

I was dizzy and disoriented as I reached to unbuckle my safety belt, and when I unlatched it, I fell onto the ceiling. Broken glass from the windshield ground into my back as I turned over and crawled out of the car.

"That sucked," I said to Samantha, who was lying next to me, gasping for breath.

"Tell me about it."

"You hurt?"

"No more than expected. I feel like I just went ten rounds with Rocky, though. At least nothing feels broken."

"Same," I said, turning over and pushing myself to my feet. I looked up to see Katie locked in battle with the murder crows. Well, it wasn't quite a battle. She was more evading the crows while they swarmed around her.

"What do we do now?" Samantha said, rising to her feet.

I looked around. We were at the top of a hill, and when I looked down, I could see our school, directly below us.

"I say we go there," I said, pointing to the school.

"Are you crazy? I don't like going to school when I have to go there."

"There are a lot of buses down there, and it's a heck of a lot safer with a bus than with a car. Don't you think?"

"Not really. They don't even have seat belts."

"It's a better idea than just staying here, so unless you come up with something better in the next five seconds, I'm going." I climbed over the guard rail and grabbed onto a tree overlooking the ledge. I looked back at Katie who clearly didn't have a better idea, and I began to slide down the hill to the school.

The hill was rocky, and my legs were torn and bleeding by the time I reached the bottom, but I survived. The school bus parking lot behind the school was protected by a chain link fence. When Samantha had fallen down the hill and landed behind me, we made our way over the fence.

Samantha looked down at her destroyed pants and glared at me. "You're paying for a new pair of pants."

"Sorry for saving your life. I'll never do it again."

"See that you don't," she said with a smile. "Except, please do."

I thought we would have to break into the school, so I was surprised when I pushed the door and it opened for me. I heard crying from the moment we opened the door, and it got louder the closer we got to the gym.

"Get ready to fight," I said.

Samantha got ready to build a fireball. "I'm ready, but I would prefer we run instead. I still don't think we can beat a coven of witches."

I inched closer to the gym and pushed open the door. There were no witches inside. Instead, I was surprised to find hundreds of people, nearly half the town, huddled in the center of the gym, on makeshift beds and using heat lamps for warmth. Out of the back of the gym, I heard a scream.

"Anna!" It was my mother, and she made a beeline right for me, wrapping me in her arms. "Oh my god. I was so worried. I thought you were dead."

"I'm not dead, Mom. I had to go find Samantha, just like I told Joanne I would."

"I nearly killed Joanne when she told me she let you go, but I didn't have time to be that angry, because a few minutes after I got home our house started to shake and this huge bright light cracked through the sky. I think it's the end of times. I really do."

I shook my head. "It's not the end of times, Mom. I'm going to fix this. I promise."

"No, you're not." She grabbed me tightly around the wrist. "You're coming with me."

I stood my ground with her. "No, Mom. You need to trust me."

"I do trust you." Her eyes filled up with tears. "I just don't want to lose you."

"You're not going to lose me, Mom."

She bowed her head. "That's what your father said."

"I'm not my father."

"No, you're not. You're brave like him, though." She shuddered and wiped tears from her eyes.

From the bleachers, I watched Joanne walk toward us. "I'm glad you're okay."

Samantha turned to us. "Is my mom here?"

Joanne turned around and pointed to the bleachers. "She's on the top bleacher. She's sleeping, but I don't think she'd mind if you woke her up."

Samantha turned to me. "We have time, right?"

I nodded. "Go."

She ran away. When she was gone, tears filled Joanne's eyes. She was looking past me, toward the door. I turned around and saw Katie there, smiling at us.

"Katie?" Joanne said, tears rolling down her cheeks. "Is that you?"

The extra magic in the air from the puncture must have made it possible for somebody without magical abilities to see Katie, because the whole town was staring at her glowing body.

"Hi, Mom." She waved. "I've missed you."

Chapter 51

I had never been so excited to eat a KIND bar than when my mother handed me one in the school gymnasium. I must have eaten it in less than five seconds, but once I'd gulped it down in far too few bites, my head started to clear. I had a lot of questions.

"How did you get to the gym?" I asked Mom.

Mom looked dazed as she thought for a moment. "The mayor called a state of emergency and evacuated everybody here. I don't know what happened, because every form of communication we have with the outside world is out of order right now, from TV to cell phones, but it wouldn't matter even if we could leave. Those stupid crows would eat us alive."

"The murder crows got to you?"

She nodded. "They picked off half a dozen of us before we got to safety. I don't know why they don't come in here and destroy us, but I guess they have better things to do."

"Yeah, like chase us."

"You saw the crows?"

I sighed deeply. "We barely escaped from them. We are only alive right now because of Katie."

Mom turned her attention to Katie, who was sitting across the gym with her mother. "I thought you were crazy. I honestly did, but everything you said was the truth, wasn't it?"

"As much as I could say." I placed my hand on hers. "I know I sounded crazy. I don't even blame you for not believing me."

Mom squeezed my hand. "I just wanted to keep you safe."

"I know, Mom, but if I learned one thing this year, it's that nobody is safe. You could die in your own room at any given moment."

"Then, maybe, if you're lucky, you'll come back. Look at Katie!"

I chuckled. "Yeah, but she just might have caused all this, too."

"How?"

I shook my head. "I'll tell you when this is all over."

I tried to stand up, but Mom pulled me back down. "Where do you think you're going?"

"I'm going to end this."

"You can't," she said, her voice desperate. "I don't want to let you out of my sight!"

I pulled my arm away. "I can't stay here. You didn't trust me before and look where it got us. Trust me now. I have to do this. Please, just let me go."

She started to cry as she stood up and wrapped her arms around me. "Just be safe, okay? Don't die. Please."

"I'll try."

I gave Mom one more long hug then walked across the bleachers to where Samantha was talking to her mother. They both had the same soft features and wild hair, except that Samantha's mom had her hair pulled back in a ponytail, and her eyes had far more age under them.

Samantha saw me walking over and waved. "Time already?"

I shrugged. "I mean, the longer we stay here, the more likely the world is going to end."

"Right." Samantha turned to her mother. "I wanted you to meet under better circumstances, but Mom, this is Anna. Anna, this is my mother."

I smiled. "It's nice to meet you. Your daughter is lovely."

"That's an interesting thing to call her. She's stubborn and hard headed, but yeah, I suppose she's lovely as well. Samantha has told me a lot about you."

"All bad, I hope."

"A little of this, and a little of that," she replied. "She said you saved her life."

"Yeah, but I also put it at risk, so there's that too."

She wrapped her arms around me. "Well, thank you for bringing her back to me."

I patted her on the back, and then pulled away. "There's a lot of that going around now, huh?"

Samantha stood up to meet us. "Mom, we have to go, just like I told you, but I'll be back."

Samantha's mom stroked her daughter's cheek. "You remember that spell I taught you, okay?"

Samantha nodded. "I will, Mom."

We turned to walk away, and I looked over at Samantha. "A new spell? I thought your dad was the witch."

"Apparently he taught my mom a thing or two. I guess if I had just opened up to her before…we have more in common than I thought."

"If only the world had ended years ago."

"Yeah, but then I wouldn't be here to stop it from ending, and that would be a travesty."

The last stop in the gym was Joanne, who stood up when she saw us and blocked our path to Katie.

"No," she said, gritting her teeth. "You're not taking her. You're not taking her again."

"Joanne," I said. "We need her help. We can't do this without her."

"I don't care. You're not taking her."

"The world's going to end," Samantha said.

Joanne wiped the tears falling down her face. "I don't care. If that's what it takes to bring my girl back to me, then let the world end."

"You're being hysterical, Mom," Katie said.

"Of course I am! You finally came back to me and I don't want you to go back there. That's not fair. None of this is fair."

"You're right," Katie replied. "None of this is fair, but life isn't fair. It sucks that I got cancer. It sucks that Dad died. It sucks that I died. And it sucks that I have to save the world now, but we just gotta deal with it."

"I don't want to deal with it," Joanne said. "How about that?"

Katie smiled at her. "Tough. Now, let me give you a ghost hug."

"What's that?"

"It's like a real hug, but you can't feel it."

"You can kind of feel the cold on your skin," I said, "but it's weird."

"Let me have my moment," Katie said, wrapping her arms around her mother.

And I did.

Chapter 52

Principal Foster led us through the dark hallways of the school and toward the main office at the front entrance. As we walked down the steps toward his office, he marched across the great seal of the school.

"I'm happy you found a friend in Samantha," the principal said over his shoulder. "I suppose I was right all along."

"Maybe don't gloat until the world is saved, huh?" I replied.

"Fair enough," he said.

Katie floated up to the great blue bear emblem on the floor but couldn't pass it. Instead, she just hovered next to it, staring down at it with a melancholy expression on her face. "This is where it all started."

I walked up to her. "I know, and this is where we're going to end it."

She looked over at me. "I'm going to miss you, you know."

I wanted to tell her that I would miss her, too, but the truth was that I still felt nothing for her. I wanted to feel what Katie felt when she looked at me, but I simply couldn't.

"I'm sure I would have missed you, too," I said.

"I wish we hadn't made that deal," she whispered.

"Then the world would end," I said. "You were right. It was our only choice."

Katie sighed. "I guess that's true, but selfishly, I don't care about that as much as I care about you."

I smiled at her. "We made our choices. Now we have to live with them."

"That's funny," Katie said. "Live with them. I know you're not trying to be funny, but that was still funny."

"Let's go," Samantha said from the door to the main office. "It's not like we have all day."

I walked with Katie into the main office. Principal Foster was behind a desk, looking through a drawer full of keys.

"This is not a sanctioned use of school property," he said, pulling out a set of keys. "However, I don't think the school board will mind, given the circumstances."

He handed the keys over to Samantha, who squeezed the keychain in her hand. "The murder crows are going to be on us immediately when we get in that cheeser."

"If you have a better idea, I'm all ears."

She smiled. "Maybe if I was a better witch I could come up with a spell, but I'm not, so I can't."

"Then it looks like we go with the first plan."

"I would tell you to be careful," Principal Foster said, "but that's impossible."

"We're going to save the world," I said to him. "It's dangerous business."

Samantha grabbed my arm and we headed out to the lot of school buses.

"Which one is ours?"

Samantha looked down at the key. "Five twenty-three."

Katie chuckled. "That's funny. That was our bus."

"I guess that Principal Foster has a sense of humor," I said

We ran up to Bus 523 and Samantha pushed open the door. Samantha took a seat in the driver's seat and I sat behind her. I dug my hands into the brown, plastic seat covers as the caws from the murder crows echoed through the bus.

"Do you know how to drive this thing?" I asked.

"It's a manual, which is what I drove in Germany, so I hope so." She turned the ignition and popped the clutch, easing into reverse. "I guess so."

I watched the murder crows turn toward us as we drove across the lot. "They're coming."

"Didn't take long."

"I'll try to distract them," Katie said. "But last time I fought them, they figured out I was just a ghost and could go right through me, so I'm not sure how long it will last."

Katie flew out the roof of the bus and into the air. I watched her through the glass as she charged heroically at the crows. "She's fearless."

Samantha changed gears as she pulled onto the street. "You would be, too, if you were already dead."

"Maybe," I said, "but I've never been that fearless about anything."

Katie rushed toward the crows, but they paid her no mind, plowing right through her on their way toward us. They reached the street in another second, and by the time we'd passed the school they were right on our tail.

"They're here," I said.

"Well, let's hope that this bus is strong enough to withstand their attack."

Katie fell through the roof. "Sorry, guys. I tried."

"It's okay." I stood up. "I think I have an idea."

There were no good ideas when you were fighting for your life, but I had an idea none the less. There was an emergency exit at the back of the bus which was big enough for me to shoot fire through. If I could get a good shot at the crows, maybe they would leave us alone, or burn up in the sky.

I rushed toward the back of the bus and kicked open the emergency door. The crows squawked at me and I stared at them for a moment. They were larger than I remembered, much bigger than the bus, and there were two of them.

"*Fiorini*," I said, closing my eyes and swirling my hands around. A small fireball formed in my hands. I opened my eyes and the ball grew wider. As it did, the crow cawed again and dived, smashing into the back of the bus and sending it swerving around the road.

I fell backwards, and in doing so my fireball exploded out the back of the bus and left a gaping hole where the emergency exit used to be.

"What are you doing?" Samantha asked. "Trying to get us killed?"

"No!" I replied. "I'm trying to save us. Just keep us straight for a second, will you?" I stood up and started to make circles with my hands again. "*Fiorini*."

This time I watched for the crow to flap and when it did, I released a fireball into the air. It slammed into the crow's face and knocked it off balance. It tumbled into the other crow behind it, and into the street.

"I think we got it!" I said.

"Good," Samantha called from the front of the bus. "Because we're almost at your house."

I couldn't believe it. We were almost to the center of the rift. With just a little more time we would be able to fix this and leave it all behind us. I couldn't enjoy the moment, though, because the birds had gotten up and were cawing loudly, their faces turned upwards. As they did, they released a magical beam into the sky.

"Oh crap," Katie said. "I forgot they could do that."

"Me too."

The crows turned their heads and directed the beam toward us. I jumped out of the way seconds before the beam slashed through the hood and cut the bus in two pieces. Samantha looked back at us in horror as the bus veered off in two different directions.

"*Proteggere!*" Samantha shouted. "I hope this works, Mom."

A blue light cradled me as I watched the other side of the bus veer into a tree and explode, just as our side fell and skidded along the ground.

It only stopped because it crashed into a house at the end of my block. I rose, wobbly, and crawled over the bus to the driver's seat. Samantha was bloody and bruised. She was bleeding from her forehead.

"Samantha!" I shouted. "Samantha!"

I shook her, but she didn't make a sound. The only sound I heard were the crows cawing loudly and flapping their wings, getting closer.

"*Finite!*" I heard a voice call from behind me.

A great bolt of red lightning crackled through the air and electrocuted the murder crows. They fell to the ground, crashing into the tree line along the way. I whipped around and squinted through the smoke and debris to see who our savior was.

It was Hilda. She was staring at us, smoke still streaming from her hands. "Well, this is a right fine mess you've gotten into this time."

Chapter 53

"Don't kill us," I said, crawling out of the overturned bus. I pulled myself over the side and fell onto the ground, where I coughed up blood.

"I'm not going to kill you, dear," she said. "You're doing a fine job of that yourself."

I rolled over and coughed again. More blood spewed out of my mouth and I felt a stabbing pain in my side.

"Why are you here?" Hilda asked.

"We're here to stop you," Katie said, floating out of the bus toward us.

"Stop me?" Hilda said, scoffing. "From what, saving the world?"

I pushed myself to my feet. "You're not saving the world. You're ending it, and we're here to make sure you can't."

Hilda started to laugh, like rightly laugh, as if she just heard the funniest joke of all time. "Oh, my dear. If I were trying to end the world, there would be nothing you could do to stop me."

"Keeping this rift open isn't going to save the world. It's going to end it," Katie said. "Have you gone mad?"

"We're not trying to keep this portal open, my dear. We're trying to close it. Who on earth told you otherwise?"

"That doesn't matter," I said, curving my hands into a ball, ready to cast the fireball spell. "Why should we believe you? You kidnapped Samantha and imprisoned her."

"We arrested her because we didn't know what you were up to, and Grendel is still a might bit irritated at you for burning down her house, I should add. Lucky for everyone involve d, I was able to reconstruct it with very little effort."

"Her mites tried to kill us."

"No, they didn't," Hilda said. "Those bugs are her guards. Still, that was a regrettable circumstance. I had no idea she was no longer using her pixies, who did a much better job than the mites." She looked at the three of us and shook her head. "We were just trying to get to the bottom of this whole thing, and frankly, we weren't sure you weren't involved in helping expand this rift in the first place. After all, you lived on the same block, and you do have a ghost familiar."

"I'm not a familiar!" Katie said. "I'm her friend."

"Yes, the dowager Vermilda told us all about it, and how you convinced her to sell her love to you for an ounce of her dragon fire."

"If you knew all of this, why didn't you stop us?"

"Well, I didn't know it until very recently now did I? In fact, not until you broke Samantha out of Grendel's pocket dimension. Once you freed Samantha, I had to learn what you were up to, and the tracking spell I placed on her clothing did the trick to tell us where you were, and tracking you down impressed upon me that you weren't evil."

"Us, evil?" Katie said. "You're the evil one."

"Oh really?" Hilda said, waving her hands in the air, until I was encircled in a yellow glow. "Then why would I save your friend?"

"Get off her!" Katie said.

Hilda snapped her fingers and the yellow exploded, sending dust into my mouth and ears. I felt the heat inside my body, and then, a searing pain in my stomach.

"Ow!" I shouted, writhing in pain.

"Stop it!" Katie said.

Hilda help up her hand and Katie flew backwards into the bus. "Stop being such a baby. It will only take a minute."

She was right. As quickly as the pain had started, it was gone, and I felt great. I pushed myself up again, and I felt like a million bucks.

"How do you feel?" Hilda said.

"Fine," I said, blinking. "Amazing, actually. What did you do to me?"

"Fixed you, of course. One of the perks of witchcraft. Now, tell me, if I was trying to kill you, why would I save you, when you were doing such a good job of killing yourself?"

"If you're not trying to kill us, then what are you doing here?"

"The Council is filled with the most powerful witches and warlocks on the planet. We spend many a day fixing rifts in the veil between our world and the Dark Place. Here we are, trying to do it again, and yet, no matter what we do, nothing can seem to close it. It's almost like there's another witch fighting to keep it open."

"The only other witch in this town is Frank."

"That you know of," Katie replied. "Frank's been trying to help us this whole time. He's given us the paste."

I felt into my pocket and pulled out the paste he gave us. I held it up for Hilda to see. "He gave us this to close the rift."

Hilda snapped her fingers and the paste appeared in her hands. She twisted off the lid and smelled it. She smiled and shook her head. "This is Elmer's glue, my dear. It can't even hold together paper very well."

My jaw dropped. "He lied to me, but why?"

"Well, it would make sense if he was up to something dastardly and wanted us distracted and fighting each other." Hilda threw up her hands. "I just can't believe it's him who's causing all of this to happen. He's a simpleton. His wife was the one with the magical prowess. There's no way he could have the power to perform such an advanced spell. There must be another explanation."

"Would a simpleton have an altar under his store? I'm new at all this, but it looked like he was performing some powerful magic to me. And he has the book. The one we got from Vermilda."

Hilda stared daggers at me. "If that's true, then we must investigate."

"When we went there, he looked as scared as we all were," Katie said. "If he's the one responsible for all of this, why would he be frightened?"

"I don't know," Hilda said. "I wrote off Frank as the culprit because I knew him to be completely devoid of magical power."

"I don't think so," I said. "He melted your golem and made a locator spell."

Hilda gritted her teeth. "It seems like I have underestimated him. Come along. We must see what Frank knows about this whole situation."

"What about Samantha?" Katie said.

"I'll summon our best healer to help her, but we must go now. Who knows what Frank is planning?" Hilda snapped her fingers and a witch, dressed in orange with a big, purple hat, appeared out of thin air. "See to the hurt one in the bus and make sure she is all right."

The witch nodded. "Yes, ma'am."

"And be quick about it. When you're done, bring her to help you." Hilda turned to me. "Shall we?"

I turned to Katie. "Stay here and make sure they take care of Samantha."

"No way," she replied. "I'm going with you."

"There's nothing you can do, ghost," Hilda said.

"So, I'm just supposed to trust you to watch out for Anna?" Katie asked, throwing her hands up.

"No," I said, taking a step closer and looking into Katie's face. "Trust me."

She teared up and looked away. "Fine, but be careful."

"I will," I turned back to Hilda. "Let's go."

Hilda nodded and snapped her fingers, and just like that we vanished from sight.

Chapter 54

We rematerialized in front of the Witch's Brew. The sky was still dark, but the light from the rift was approaching the strip mall quickly and seemed to increase with each passing second.

"The rift will be over the store in a couple of minutes. Then, we won't be able to stop whatever Frank has planned."

"How do we stop him?"

Hilda walked to the door. "I don't know. That depends on what he's planning. But if we don't stop him, who knows what he will unleash on this planet."

"Should we really be going in there with just the two of us?"

"No," Hilda said. "But aside from the one helping your friend, Samantha, it's taking every ounce of mana we have just to keep this darkness from spreading."

Hilda placed her hand on the door and an explosion pushed her backwards toward the street. She pushed herself up and brushed herself off. "This is old magic. Nothing that a simpleton like Frank could command. *Hexious Revil.*"

She waved her hand across the building, and a giant orange orb revealed itself. Letters and symbols floated around the translucent orb encasing the door.

"It is as I feared. These wards are almost ancient in their construction. These spells are buried deep in the central branch of the library. There's no way he could have known about them without help."

"Can you break them?" I asked.

"Well, of course. Even old magic is not immune to blunt force. *Tilforcian Blazian Ugmendo.*"

Hilda held out her arms in front of her, and a giant beam of blue light shot out and blasted into the orange orb. It seemed to be able to take the force of the blast without being destroyed, but then Hilda's eyes glowed white, and the beam intensified. The orb bent and cracked, until it exploded and shattered into a million pieces. The shards vanished.

"There," Hilda said, straightening her blue coat. She walked forward, grabbed the handle, and whispered something I couldn't understand. The knob glowed red before it fell off entirely, and the door swung open. "In we go."

Inside, barbed wire still lined the floor, glowing in many different colors. Hilda held me back as I walked inside. She closed her eyes and muttered something under her breath. Then, she snapped her fingers and wisps of purple smoke came out of her mouth. As the wisps snaked around the room, the barbed wires exploded, leaving nothing but singe marks where the wires had been.

Hilda pushed her arms apart and the purple wisps became blue lights that led the way through the room. She stepped forward confidently and pushed open the door to the back room with the slightest nudge of her fingers.

"We mustn't dawdle, Anna," she said. "Time is of the essence."

"You just moved through those barbs like it was nothing."

"Of course I did, dear. Those spells I have seen before, and when you have seen everything, nothing scares you. You could learn it too someday, if you weren't so headstrong. I can see your magical aura now, where it was lost to me before."

"Who says I want to learn it?"

"I suppose nobody, actually, except for everybody in the world. I've never met somebody who didn't want to be a witch or a warlock." Hilda pressed on the back wall, but nothing happened. "How does this all work to get down to the subbasement?"

"I don't know," I said. "He closed the door and we just fell."

"Ah," she said, walking back across the room and closing the door. "Of course. *Belonius.*"

The room started to shake and began to shoot downward more quickly than it had the last time. My stomach moved into my mouth, and I wanted to vomit. Luckily, the room stopped right before I was about to spew chunks.

"This way," Hilda said, opening the door.

"It's the only way," I said blankly. But I followed her.

"Unless we want to go back the way we came, you are correct, though I have no interest in returning to the store. Do you?"

I shook my head. "No."

"Good. Then we must press onwards until the end."

The door led to a craggy stairwell, just like I had seen before when Frank led us down to his altar. However, the rocks somehow felt closer than they had before, and as we moved down the steps, they seemed to close in on us.

"That is just an illusion, dear," Hilda said. "All of this is very clever, but it is nothing but smoke and mirrors."

At the bottom of the stairs we came to the rock door with no lever or handle. Hilda pressed her hand against it. When she couldn't open it with her hands, she turned to me.

"How did he get in here?"

"He pressed his hand on the wall and said something. I don't remember the spell."

"I very much doubt that. If you want to become a witch, you must remember. A witch never forgets a spell. Well, think. Think, think."

"This is the kind of thing Katie would remember."

"We don't have Katie. We have you."

"I think it was *Emegtu…Ligotiu…Reanta.*"

Hilda sighed loudly to convey her disappointment. "You think, or you know?"

"I think," I said, my voice trembling.

"Well, I suppose it will have to do." She placed her hand on the door. "Just like this?"

"Yes."

"*Emegtu Ligotiu Reanta,*" she said.

The green light shone on Hilda, and when it was done scanning her up and down, it turned red.

"That's not good," Hilda said.

There was a thundering crack on the stairwell, and the rocks fell onto the ground. As they did, they cracked and broke open, revealing rock monsters underneath. Their eyes glowed red and they moved toward Hilda, their legs smashing into the ground with each laborious step.

"Perhaps I was wrong about the illusions. But we don't have time for this," Hilda said. "*Evapori.*"

A great wave of energy crashed out from Hilda, and the rock monsters cracked in half and fell down, dead. As the rock figures crumbled, so did the door. It split down the middle and fell open, revealing the green light oozing out from inside.

"That was easier than I thought," Hilda said. "But harder than I hoped."

Hilda disappeared inside the room, and I followed, worried about what we would find but happy to have somebody as strong as Hilda on my side.

Chapter 55

Green light emanated from every crevice inside the room. The shelves along the walls that once held different body parts were all empty, and Frank stood behind the altar, chanting and screaming.

"Hades, great god of the underworld! I call to you!"

Surrounding him on the altar were the dozens of jars missing from the shelves around the room. In the center of the altar was the dragon fire, still burning brightly. Frank began to unscrew its lid, but Hilda ran forward.

"No!" she shouted.

Frank swung his hand, and Hilda rose into the air with his motion. "Ah, so nice of you to come, Mrs. Feffernoose. It's not a party without you."

"I know what you are doing, Frank, and you can't bring her back."

"Of course I can!" Frank shouted. "You told me how, all those years ago."

"I told you nothing. My lessons were meant for Gina's ears only."

"Yes," he said, beckoning her to come closer, and she hovered ever closer at his command. "Everything you said was for Gina, and yet, I heard it too. You thought I was too stupid to put it all together, but I wasn't. Now, I have it all, without your help."

"No!" I shouted. "With mine."

Frank smiled. "Ah, my little protégé. Yes, with your help, too. Together, we have the means to bring back my dear wife, and once we've done that, we can bring back your friend as well."

"That's crazy!" I said, stepping forward. "You're going to destroy the world!"

"A small price to pay to be reunited with my beloved. I've waited years for a rift to open close by so that I could use it, and now it has come! I will not be denied!"

I shook my head. "But they're not the same when they come back, not after so long. Katie told me—"

"What does she know?" Frank shouted. "I have studied this my whole life, and she has been dead for days."

"It's true," Hilda said. "My lessons to Gina were a theoretical construct designed around a ghost who was still on Earth, unable to move on. You can't bring back somebody from the rift. Not when they've been dead as long as Gina has been."

"Liar!" Frank bellowed. He hurled his arm through the air, and sent Hilda crashing into the empty shelves. Then he turned his attention to me. "Don't listen to them. Don't listen to anyone. We can do it."

"I don't want to do it. Katie wouldn't want this. Gina wouldn't want this."

"How do you know?" Frank shouted. "You never knew her." He bowed his head. "We would have been married for twenty years this month. It's been so hard without her."

"It's supposed to be hard!" I screamed, moving closer. "That's what this whole thing is about, this life! It's hard."

"You know nothing, little girl!" Frank said, raising his arm. With it, my body rose into the air. With the flick of his wrist he sent me flying into the same shelf as Hilda, and when I hit the ground those shelves came crashing down on both of us.

"Hades! God of the underworld!" Frank said, tilting his head back. "I summon you!"

A bolt of lightning crashed through the room. I closed my eyes to avoid the flash, and when I looked again there was a charred spot where the lightning had struck. In front of it, a tall, bearded, dark-skinned man, almost as tall as the room itself, ambled forward. He was dressed in a toga and carried a golden sword in his hand.

"Who dares summon me?" the man's voice thundered through the room.

"I do," Frank said. "Great god of the underworld. I summon you, Hades."

"He did it," Hilda said, groggily. "He summoned Hades."

"You puny mortal," Hades said, stepping up to the altar. "You dare evoke my name in prayer and demand I come to you?"

"I do, oh lord, for a great purpose," Frank said, bowing to Hades.

"And what purpose would this be?" Hades said.

"I have arranged all the ingredients needed to bring back my dear, departed Gina. She was taken from me, and only you have the power to bring her back."

"Is that why you have caused so much chaos in my underworld, mortal? To save the one you love?"

"Yes, my dark god. I only wish to have returned that which was taken from me."

Hades studied the ingredients on the altar. "You have collected a fine list of items. However, I cannot help you."

"Cannot, or will not?"

"Both, and neither. Your wife no longer is your wife. She has been drained of her essence and reconstituted in a new form."

"I don't understand."

Hades rolled his eyes. "She has been reincarnated into a little boy in Cameroon."

"You lie!" Frank said. "Why does everyone lie to me?"

"I do not lie!" Hades screamed loud enough to make the room quake. "I should turn you into a sea sponge for the mere implication."

Frank sniffled, starting to cry. "I have done everything required of me, and it is still not enough?"

Hades nodded. "I'm afraid even the best of humanity will never be enough."

"I want to be with her again," Frank said, dropping his head.

"I cannot make that happen in this life, but I can reunite you again in the next."

Frank looked up. "You can?"

"If that is your request."

Frank nodded. "Yes, please."

"Then let it be done."

Hades snapped his fingers and Frank vanished in an instant, leaving nothing behind, except for his altar full of body parts locked in jars.

Chapter 56

I pushed the shelf off me and stood up to lift it so Hilda could climb out as well. Hades paced across the altar.

"Now that's over," he said, brushing his hands off on his toga, "maybe it's time for a froyo. Persephone would like one, I'm sure. What was the flavor she liked so much?" He stopped and pointed to me. "You, girl. Where is there a frozen yogurt stand around here?"

I froze to the spot. "Um, there's one about a mile away from here, on Frontier and Main."

Hades squinted suspiciously. "Is it any good?"

"It's all right," I said. "It's no Red Mango, but it's pretty okay."

"Thank you," he said. "You are most kind."

"Wait," I said. "You can't just leave."

He turned to me. "Of course I can. Haven't you heard? I'm a god, and we can do anything we want. Why, my father once turned into a horse and fought a camel. It was quite entertaining."

"No," I said. "I don't mean you can't leave. I meant…please don't leave. There's so much we have to fix, and we could really use your help."

Hades stepped down from the altar. "Yes, I suppose there is a bit of a mess down here, isn't there. I'm not sure what you want me to do about it."

"Can't you…fix it?"

He scratched his head. "Well, I'd love to help, but it's just, well, I don't know how. I'm not very good at this type of thing. That's why my father created magic, to allow witches to do that kind of work for us."

Hilda stepped forward. "We have the ingredients to make a paste which should close the portal."

"The paste," Hades said, smacking himself on the head. "Of course. How silly of me." He snapped his fingers and the ingredients on the altar combined into a single jar, full of white paste. "There you go. Now if you'll excuse me—"

"Is Frank really gone?" I asked.

Hades nodded. "Of course, little girl."

"And his wife was really reincarnated?"

Hades smiled. "That's what happens when you die. You're left in the Dark Place until you forget everything about your life, and then you start over, with a new soul. Making souls costs an incredible amount of mana but recycling them into new hosts takes very little."

"And my friend, Katie, she'll forget all about me, won't she?"

Hades nodded. "Yes, and you'll forget about her, too, but then, you'll start over, and maybe you'll meet again."

"Do you really think so?"

Hades smiled. "I'll make a note of it. In your next lives, I promise you will have more time together."

Hilda walked up the stairs to the altar. She picked up the jar and brought it back down to Hades. "Here. You'll need this."

Hades shook his head. "Oh no. I can't fix the rift. Or, more appropriately, I won't. That's witch's work. Now, if you'll excuse me…froyo." Hades snapped his fingers and vanished.

Hilda shook her head. "Ugh. Gods. They are the worst. We don't need him, anyway. Now that we have the paste we need, it should be an easy patch job."

She was right. With Frank not actively working to keep the portal open, the witches made quick work of fixing it with the paste and soon there was nothing but a little hole left, which rested right over the clearing in the woods where Katie had first brought me.

Once Katie had gone through it, the witches would close it for good. We all met there, when it was almost over, and the witches had finished their work to close the puncture between our world and the Dark Side.

"I don't want to go," Katie said, looking through the hole. "I always knew I would have to go, but now that it's come, I don't want to do it."

"I wish I could hug you," Joanne said to her, sobbing.

"It's okay, Mom," she said. "Maybe we'll be together in another life."

"I hope so."

Katie floated over to Samantha. "I think it was cool that you helped me, even though you didn't have to."

"I think it's cool that you're a ghost," Samantha replied.

Katie looked over at me, still speaking to Samantha. "Take care of her for me, okay?"

"I will," Samantha promised, wiping a tear from her cheek.

"I don't need anybody to take care of me."

"Yes, you do." Katie faced me now. "Everybody needs somebody looking out for them."

"I wish I felt bad about you leaving," I said to Katie. "I know I should feel bad, but I just don't feel anything."

"About that," Hilda said, walking up to me from the portal. "Hades gave me something for you." She held out her hand, and a yellow ball of light floated in it. "This is the love you had for Katie. Hades found it in the underworld, and told me to give it back to you, if you wanted it."

"You don't have to take it," Katie said. "Maybe it's better that you don't miss me."

I shook my head, grabbing the ball of light from Hilda's hand. "I want to miss you. I want that pain. It's part of loving you, and I'll never feel bad about that."

I dragged the orb close to me. I knew exactly what to do without having to be told. I pushed it against my chest, and it absorbed into me. Suddenly, a flood of emotions came flooding back, and I fell to my knees, crying.

"It will take a minute to readjust," Hilda said. "It's like having a week's worth of emotions come at you all at once."

I pressed my hands on the ground and breathed deeply. Looking up at Katie, I remembered everything, every emotion and every feeling that ever went into knowing her. It was pure pain, but wonderful pain. When I stood up again, I was sobbing uncontrollably.

"Do you regret it?" Katie asked. "Taking back your emotions?"

"Not one bit."

"It's time to go," Hilda said to Katie. "If you want to go back, the time is now."

Katie nodded. "Okay."

"Are you sure you want to go back?" I said. "You can still stay here, with me."

"No," Katie said. "You have to move on, and so do I." She leaned forward and placed her lips on mine. I felt the cold come off her mouth, and I closed my eyes.

"I love you," she said, and then the cold was gone. I opened my eyes. The rift was closed, and there was no Katie.

I turned to Hilda. "Can I ask you a question?"

"Anything, dear," Hilda replied.

"Am I cursed?"

Hilda cocked her head to one side. "What ever do you mean, dear?"

I sighed. "Almost everybody I've ever loved is dead."

The witch shook her head. "That doesn't mean you're cursed, dear. You're just having a bit of any unlucky life, but things can always turn around."

"Well, that's good to know, I guess."

"Come on," Samantha said, throwing an arm over my shoulder. "I'll buy you lunch."

I smiled. "I'm not that hungry…froyo sounds good, though."

Author Notes

This book was originally supposed to be a comic book script. My friend asked me to pitch him something, but nothing I showed him was working. Even after multiple tries, nothing clicked for me.

Then, I traveled to Worldcon in San Jose, and as I was going to sleep in another friend's guest bed, I had this idea. I shot up from bed in the middle of the night and furiously typed out the beginning of what would become *Anna and the Dark Place*. It was super rough, but even then, I loved it so much.

This is what I wrote to him.

Susie Against the Dark Place

Susie Jenkins's best friend, Teresa, died last week. She's been taking it poorly, so when Teresa comes to her at night as a ghost and tells her the barrier between the Dark Place and Earth is breaking down, Susie is skeptical at best.

At first, Susie is sure she is having a mental break, but slowly, after many doctor visits, Susie begins to believe Teresa is real. With her friend's help, Susie sets out to become a witch so she can save the world.

As the book goes on, Susie and Teresa carry on like old friends. While studying, Susie begins to realize if she is successful, Teresa will be gone forever. This sends her into a second grief spiral, where she contemplates letting the world end so she can keep her

*friend around. However, she eventually
comes to term with her friend's death, learns
how to mend the hole in the barrier and her
heart, and say goodbye to her friend
forever.*

*It's a story about grief, loss, friendship, and
how you say goodbye to a friend without
ever leaving them behind.*

*The Dark Place, in this case, has two
meanings, b/c Susie is fighting against the
literal dark place within us all, and against
The Dark Place, the void where souls go
after they die.*

The gist of the story remained, though obviously I changed her name.

My YA books have always been about death, grief, and loss, but I had never tackled the love between two friends before, which is what makes *Anna and the Dark Place* so special.

Yes, they fell in love, too, but at the base level they are good friends with a deep and lasting friendship. That's what I wanted to explore in this book—what it's like to lose somebody that means so much to you.

The book didn't originally have mythological creatures in it, but I just love them so much that I couldn't avoid putting them into the story. I love the idea of these two friends gathering these pieces to a potion and having to work through their grief in the process.

Originally, Frank wasn't the bad guy, either. It was Hilda, but that felt too on the nose. Besides, the real "bad guy" was Death. It took Frank and Anna's loves away from them, and that's the real battle in this book.

I won't say the book stayed on outline, because no outline survives the first draft, but the broad strokes remained…until the end. The end was totally different from what I imagined.

It was originally a much smaller book, but it kept ballooning up on me. Anna was just going to close the portal, and be done with it, with no heightened drama, and definitely no murder crows.

And what would this book be without murder crows?

Or the dust mite guardians of the pocket dimension.

The thing I love about books is that even though I'm the one writing them, they still surprise even me. It's a long and tedious process to write a book, so it's a nice feeling when they manage to sneak up on you, which they always do at least once in a book. It makes me feel almost like I am a reader of my own work.

*

I hope you liked *Anna and the Dark Place*. If you did, check out *The Void Calls Us Home*. It's a Lovecraftian YA novel about a girl dealing with the darkness inside of her, while getting over the loss of her sister.

*

Now, here is a preview of *The Void Calls Us Home*.

The Void Calls Us Home

By:

Russell Nohelty

Edited by:

Leah Lederman

Proofread by:

Katrina Roets

Cover by:
Paramita Bhattacharjee

Rebecca,

I can't do this anymore. I tried everything. The call is too great. It's too strong. It hounds me at all hours of the day and night. It consumes my every waking thought.

It will never let me go.

I have tried to deny it. I have tried to drown it out, but it is too much. It calls me to it. It calls me home. I must heed the call and return to the Void. I love you so much.

Goodbye.

Mary

Chapter 1

I have never been suicidal.

Sure, I've had dark thoughts in my life, but who hasn't? They were never more than just a passing thought that swooped into my mind and left as quickly as they came. I was a relatively happy human female, all things considered, and yet…

I think I tried to kill myself last night. I hate using the word "think". I mean, if I tried to kill myself, that's the kind of thing I should know, right?

It is, but that didn't change the fact I just wasn't sure.

God, that sounded so moronic. Even stupider than it sounded rattling around in my brain. It's just that, one moment, I was driving along, minding my own business. And then, I was off the side of the road, plummeting down an embankment, and slamming into a tree. The rest of the car ride I remembered vividly, but that last moment...

The reason that I jerked the wheel to the right on that lonely, dark, mountain road…that's what was fuzzy.

I remembered singing along to Kesha's "Rainbow", where she goes, "I've found a rainbow, rainbow, baby Trust me, I know, life is scary, but just put those colors on, girl. Come and play along with me tonight…" Suddenly the temperature in my car plummeted. The hair on my arms stood up on end and I felt as if my insides were being hollowed out, as if every good thought in my body had been stripped away from me.

I stopped singing. I stopped everything and stared blankly out into the dark night. It was rainy, and the thick drops fell onto my windshield. The wipers whipped across

the glass as they struggled to keep the water at bay. I
should have replaced them months ago, but it always
slipped my mind.

The music must have still been on right before the car
jerked to the right, but I couldn't hear it anymore. All I
heard was the rhythmic wiping of the windshield as I
peered out into the dark beyond my headlights. The
darkness hypnotized me. Hopelessness washed over me,
utter hopelessness; despair that felt eternal.

Then, I spun my wheel to the right…

…and I fell…

When my head slammed into the steering wheel, the
darkness engulfed me. I drifted through the nothing like
some dark, underwater pit, except that I wasn't drowning. I
wasn't gasping for breath. I wasn't even frightened. I was
one with the black. Without hope, fear, or happiness. I
just…was.

I heard the muffled sounds of the medics prying me
from the car, and later the voices of doctors as they worked
to save my life, but I couldn't see them. I couldn't feel
them. I was numb, completely and utterly without feeling,
left with nothing but the frigid cold.

I don't know how long I floated in the emptiness. I
swam in every direction, looking for a flicker of warmth
that eluded me. I longed for comfort, for heat, for answers,
but no matter how far I travelled, there was nothing around
me. I screamed into the abyss, but there was nobody there.

Without warning, a great force jerked me by the throat
and pulled me out of the darkness. I woke up gasping for
breath. My eyes fluttered opened, and I sucked in oxygen
as if I had come back from drowning.

Nurses and doctors flooded into the room as I spasmed
uncontrollably on the bed, kicking off the fresh linens. A

needle jabbed in my arm, and then, it was quiet again. This time, I did not fall into the hopeless void, but into a pleasant dream, where I was a pony.

The second time I woke, my eyes focused on my mother. She looked as though she hadn't slept in days. Her short, blonde hair was tangled, and her face was greasy. Dark circles rested under her eyes. I hadn't seen her without make-up once in my entire life, and the sight was enough to jar me awake.

"Mom?" I asked, weakly. I tried to push myself to my elbows, but the pain in my chest burned and I collapsed back onto the hospital bed like a ten-ton rock.

"Becca!" Mom said, her voice cracking with excitement. "Becca! You're awake!"

She jumped up and wrapped her arms around my neck. She pressed herself closely and my chest throbbed again.

"Ow," I said to her. My mother was not an emotional person by any stretch of the imagination. I couldn't remember her ever hugging me like that, and yet she held me so tight I thought I would burst.

"Sorry," Mom said, pushing herself back and wiping the tears from her eyes. "I didn't know if I would ever see you again."

"It's okay," I said, taking a deep heave of air. Every breath was agony, but I couldn't stop taking long inhales and exhales, enjoying my breath in a way I never had before. "How long have I been…how long have I been out?"

"Four weeks," she replied. "They told me you would never wake up, but I knew. I just knew that you would. I…knew."

Mom swallowed her sadness as the tears came again. Mom hadn't even cried at my sister's funeral, and yet here she was, sobbing at my bedside. She tried to talk but it was no use. All that eked out where mumbled syllables that I couldn't understand. She collapsed back onto the chair and wept into her hands.

"You're up!" I heard from the doorway.

I turned my aching head to see my father standing at the door with two cups of coffee. He was a big man, and broad. He could have played linebacker in the NFL with his massive size, except that he had the coordination of a running camel.

"Hi, Dad," I replied, groggy. "Ignore Mom. She's having a moment."

Dad smiled at me. "She's emotional, kiddo."

"I know," I said. "I don't know what to do. This is a foreign experience to me."

"Just give her a minute."

He barreled forward to give me a hug, but I held out my hand to stop him. My arms throbbed as they swung above my body.

"Please, no," I said. "I don't think my body can take one of your bear hugs right now."

He shrugged, disappointed but understanding. My father was not emotionally stilted like my mother. He was responsible for most of the affection I received in my life. My sister accounted for the rest, but…

"I get it," he said, holding up his hand. "I'm just, oh, I'm really glad to see you, is all." He leaned forward to place a gentle kiss on my forehead.

My vision swirled and crackled, and my eyes turned up into my head. I tried to keep my head up, but it was no use. I collapsed back in bed and drifted off, hoping I would dream of kittens and not the black nothingness I had been trapped in for so long.

Chapter 2

I drifted in and out of consciousness for the next three days. When I was awake, the pain was excruciating, but being asleep was even worse. When I was asleep, I was haunted by an image.

It was a thousand-foot-high black eye, sucking blue and orange flames into itself from every direction. It searched for me in the darkness, but it could not find me, no matter where it looked. I waved my arms, desperate for it to see me, but it did not. It was a nightmare, not because it searched for me, but because it couldn't find me.

I wanted desperately for the flaming eye to see me. I called out to it, begging for its warmth to save me from the cold darkness, but when it turned to my direction, it only looked through me, no matter how much I screamed and flailed my arms.

I might have chalked up my recurring dreams to just that, crazy dreams, if I wasn't remembering more about my crash with each passing day.

That flaming eye…

I had seen it before. I didn't remember it when I first woke up, but the longer I was awake, the more I remembered…

It had flashed in front of my eyes the moment before I jerked my car off the road. It was the reason I swerved off the mountain in the first place. It had beckoned me toward it, and I desperately wanted to answer the call. After I slipped into a coma, I searched for it in the darkness. It was my salvation, and yet, it had abandoned me.

I didn't know I why wanted the flaming eye to take me away. I led a good life, a charmed life even; a life that I loved. I went to a great school, lived in a beautiful house, and already had three offers to Ivy League schools in my junior year of high school.

I'm privileged. Not everybody got the chance to play on the varsity basketball team, and even few could still pull straight A's while doing it. I wasn't trying to brag, mind you, just explaining that I totally understand how lucky I was. Depression couldn't have been the reason I pulled my car off the road. I wasn't depressed.

"Good afternoon, Ms. Rose." A short, squat doctor with frizzy, red hair walked into my room. "I'm Doctor Montrell. How are you doing this afternoon?"

"Fine, doctor," I lied.

"Don't sound too confident," Doctor Montrell replied. "I mean, you're alive. That must account for something, and conscious, which in and of itself is a bit of a miracle."

"I'm in a lot of pain," I said. "But I'm trying to keep a stiff upper lip about it. Still sucks though."

"Yeah, it does, and it's okay to think your situation sucks," Doctor Montrell said. She was flipping through pages on my chart. "I mean, you really hurt yourself. It's okay to admit that to me, all right. I need to know the truth. Understand?"

I hung my head. "Yes, doctor."

"Good. Now is there anything you need to tell me?"

"No, doctor."

"You don't sound too confident."

I wasn't confident. I wanted more than anything to tell somebody about the flaming eye in my dreams and figure out why I wanted to kill myself and join it. I'm young, bright, and generally positive, most of the time. Some people might even call me a ball of freaking sunshine, and yet…I had tried to kill myself.

But I couldn't tell her anything, could I? Not yet. At least not without having my sanity questioned. I needed to get out of the hospital first, and then maybe I could find some answers.

"My head just hurts a lot," I said.

"Well, that's normal after suffering a severe concussion. You'll feel better with time."

"Thanks," I replied. "Hey, Doc. When am I gonna be able to go home?"

"Let's get you up and walking around, and then we'll see about sending you home, okay?"

I smiled, even though it hurt my bruised cheeks. "Okay."

"Your physical therapist will be in shortly," Doctor Montrell said, walking toward the door. "Be honest with her about your pain levels, okay? Don't try to push yourself. She holds your future in her hands. You don't leave until she says it's okay."

The doctor left, and I fell back into bed, trembling in pain. Even with the painkillers, I still felt the sting in my chest every time I moved.

I tried to remember how lucky I was. It could have been much worse. I broke my arm, bruised three ribs, and snapped my nose when I slammed my head into the steering wheel, but I wasn't dead. By all accounts, I should have been.

*

If you liked this, make sure to pick up *The Void Calls Us Home* today.

ALSO BY RUSSELL NOHELTY

THE GODVERSE CHRONICLES
And Death Followed Behind Her
And Doom Followed Behind Her
And Ruin Followed Behind Her
And Hell Followed Behind Her
Katrina Hates the Dead
Pixie Dust

OTHER NOVEL WORK
My Father Didn't Kill Himself
Sorry for Existing
Gumshoes: The Case of Madison's Father
The Invasion Saga
The Vessel
Worst Thing in the Universe
The Void Calls Us Home
The Marked Ones
The Sleeping Beauty

OTHER ILLUSTRATED WORK
The Little Bird and the Little Worm
Ichabod Jones: Monster Hunter
Gherkin Boy

www.russellnohelty.com

www.wannabepress.com

www.ingramcontent.com/pod-product-compliance
Lightning Source LLC
Chambersburg PA
CBHW071139180726
48291CB00007B/2247